See You
Soon,
Samantha

SUMMER · APPLE · CANDY · APPLE · SUMMER

candy apple books... just for you.

The Accidental Cheerleader by Mimi McCoy

The Boy Next Door by Laura Dower

Miss Popularity by Francesco Sedita

How to Be a Girly Girl in Just Ten Days
by Lisa Papademetriou

Drama Queen by Lara Bergen

The Babysitting Wars by Mimi McCoy

Totally Crushed by Eliza Willard

I've Got a Secret by Lara Bergen

Callie for President by Robin Wasserman

Making Waves by Randi Reisfeld and H. B. Gilmour

The Sister Switch
by Jane B. Mason and Sarah Hines Stephens

Accidentally Fabulous by Lisa Papademetriou

Confessions of a Bitter Secret Santa by Lara Bergen

Accidentally Famous by Lisa Papademetriou

Star-Crossed by Mimi McCoy

Accidentally Fooled by Lisa Papademetriou

Miss Popularity Goes Camping by Francesco Sedita

Life, Starring Me! by Robin Wasserman

Juicy Gossip by Erin Downing

Accidentally Friends by Lisa Papademetriou

Snowfall Surprise
by Jane B. Mason and Sarah Hines Stephens

The Sweetheart Deal by Holly Kowitt

Rumor Has It by Jane B. Mason and Sarah Hines Stephens

Super Sweet 13 by Helen Perelman

Wish You Were Here, Liza by Robin Wasserman

See You Soon, Samantha

by Lara Bergen

SCHOLASTIC INC.

New York   Toronto   London   Auckland
Sydney   Mexico City   New Delhi   Hong Kong

No part of this publication may be reproduced, stored in a retrieval system, or transmitted in any form or by any means, electronic, mechanical, photocopying, recording, or otherwise, without written permission of the publisher. For information regarding permission, write to Scholastic Inc., Attention: Permissions Department, 557 Broadway, New York, NY 10012.

ISBN 978-0-545-17223-3

12 11 10 9 8 7 6 5 4   12 13 14 15/0

Printed in the U.S.A.   40
First printing, June 2010

To everyone who lives for summer vacation

Chapter One

Ride, ride, ride.
Ridin' in the car, car, car.
Drive, drive, drive.
I swear I've never driven so far.
I don't even know
how far I gotta go.
I just know that it's far . . .
and I really have to pee . . .

Okay, so I don't know if this is one of the best songs I've ever written. But it was the best I could do in my situation: stuck with a bulging bladder in the backseat of our old station wagon, somewhere between my house in New Jersey and a beach in

North Carolina where I'd be spending the next — gulp! — two months of my life.

Thank goodness we needed gas and could finally stop for a bathroom break after five hours. (My mom was a driving machine!)

The fact that I was stuck in the backseat *without* the new guitar that I'd gotten for my twelfth birthday a week before probably didn't help my songwriting much either. Talk about unfair! And no, it was not in the trunk or tied to the roof of the car, where I'd quite patiently explained to my parents that it should be. It was back at home in my room because, as my mom quite *im*patiently explained to me, I was insane if I thought she was going to haul that enormous thing I didn't even know how to play yet across four states. She was having a hard enough time cramming two months' worth of stuff into our clunky old car, anyway.

"Do you really have to bring two pairs of combat boots?" she actually asked me.

Hello! How could I be Goth (my awesome new twelve-year-old look) without them?

"Definitely, Mom," I told her. "These pink ones go with the outfit I'm wearing for the trip." (One pink-and-black-checked hoodie and an extremely cute black tutu skirt.) "And the black ones are for every day, thank you very much."

Even though I had to leave it behind, I was still psyched to have gotten the guitar at all. Especially after my mom kept reminding me how much I'd begged her and my dad for birthday gifts like ballet lessons . . . and a skateboard . . . and a hamster . . . and yeah, maybe a million other things — and how little interest I had in those things now. (Don't worry — the hamster's now loving life with Carole Anne, my neighbor who still takes ballet.) In fact, before my birthday, I'd pretty much geared myself up for getting some totally boring clothes — which could hopefully be exchanged for something cute and very Goth.

But my parents came through again!

(Plus, my dad said he'd bring my guitar when he joined us at the beach in two weeks.)

In the meantime, I had something else to keep me sane: my trusty iPod, headphones, and a fully charged battery. Do not leave home on a gazillion-mile car trip without them. Unless, of course, you actually *enjoy* listening to your mother sing along to show tunes for hours at the top of her lungs, or hearing your little brother's play-by-play of what-ever annoying DS game he's glued to. (I, for one, do not.)

What I *do* like is finding a great new song, put-ting it on repeat, and listening to it over and over and over again. After a while, every note and every lyric completely soaks into me just like one of those miracle sponges you see on TV — without anyone telling me to stop already, I'm driving them crazy. (And by "anyone," I mean my mom . . . and even my BFFs, Mina and Liza, sometimes.) That's the best, if you ask me. After a while, it's almost like I'm not listening to the song anymore. I just *am* the song.

Then I usually get sick of it, and move on to the next one.

I hope one day I can write a song that someone wants to listen to again and again and again. . . .

So anyway, I had my new songs — thanks to one set of grandparents who'd given me a gift card that I used for twenty new downloads for my birthday — so I was in pretty good shape. Plus, I had a fresh *Tiger Beat*, *J-14*, and *Seventeen*, which I was dying to dig into (thank you very much, birthday money from other grandparents!). I had souvenirs for Liza and Mina to think about, too, since we'd promised to send one another something crazy and special while we were all away. And of course, I had the beach to look forward to.

In fact, I think if my annoying little brother, Josh, hadn't insisted on letting his elbow touch my pillow — gross! — it might have been a down-right pleasant trip.

And to think that when my mom first told us about her whole summer plan, I'd totally dreaded it.

"Guess what!" my mom had said that night at the dinner table.

"Chicken butt!" yelped my brother. (He's nine. That's what he does. When will my mother learn?)

"Tell us, Mom," I said.

"Well," she began, flashing a goofy, giddy grin. (My mom can be so weird, I swear.) "Karen Abelard called today!"

"Uh . . . cool . . ." I told her. "So what's for dessert?"

"Strawberries," said my mom. "And that's not the cool part."

I think I groaned then for two reasons: One, I do not consider *strawberries* "dessert"; and two, how "cool" can anything be that begins with "Karen Abelard called today"?

Karen Abelard, you should know, is one of my mom's best friends from college. They were room-mates, and bridesmaids at each other's weddings. I have to say, I'm constantly amazed that they're

BFFs. I mean, my mom is not cool — she wears Christmas socks (in *May*!), and refuses to wear makeup (what's the point of being a grown-up?), and has all these mortifying old pictures of herself that she insists on posting on Facebook (think sweatshirts with shoulder pads, then add a pair of GIANT glasses). But Karen Abelard is *so* not cool. I mean, she's nice ... but a little out there. She's from North Carolina, and she's really into yoga, strange jewelry, and *extremely* ugly shoes. Plus, she has this crazy accent. And her husband, Jay? He's just plain weird.

So whatever, she called. Big deal. I wanted ice cream.

"We're going to spend the whole summer with her at the beach!" my mom said.

"What?!" I gasped. To be honest, it's a miracle that I'm still here to tell this story, since I practically choked on my last sugar snap pea.

"Chicken butt!" said my brother.

"Would you be quiet?" I said. Then I turned back to my mother. "Did you say the *whole* summer? With the real-life 'fairly odd parents'?!" Karen and her family had stayed with us for one night on their way to Vermont back in the fall, and that was quite enough for me.

My mom sighed and gave me one of those looks she just *loves* to give. "Sam," she said. "They are wonderful people. It'll be fun. And I exaggerated. It's not the whole summer . . . exactly."

I let out a sigh, too relieved to even bother to remind her for the zillionth time to call me Samantha now, and not Sam, please.

"Just July and August," she added.

"Mom!" I moaned. "What are you trying to do? Destroy my life?" I asked her. "And my name is Sam*antha*, remember?"

"Liza and Mina call you Sam. I just heard them today," Josh spoke up.

"That's different," I replied, shooting him a glare.

"Okay, *Samantha*," my mom said, nodding. "Now, how would a summer at the beach destroy your life?"

"Let me count the ways," I said very calmly. I held up my hand and raised my carefully black-Magic-Markered fingers one by one. (So Goth, I know.) "One," I said, "I'll miss Liza. Two, I'll miss Mina. Three, I'll miss Jeremy Ryan. And four . . . Olivia Miner will steal Jeremy Ryan away while I'm gone!"

My mom sighed, reached out, and gently folded

down fingers one and two. "I thought Mina and Liza were going away for the summer, also," she said. "Remember? Liza's driving across the country with her family, and Mina's going to art camp in New York." Then she pointed to fingers three and four. "And who is Jeremy Ryan?"

"*Oooh*, Jeremy Ryan ... Sam's *boy*friend ..." Josh made some disgusting kissing sounds, which compelled me to punch him in the arm.

"He is not my boyfriend," I said to my mom. "But he is the cutest, most amazing boy in school and I bet he *could* be my boyfriend if you didn't drag me to the ends of the earth for the entire summer."

"Salt Isle, North Carolina, is not the ends of the earth," said my mom. "And I thought you liked Myles Porter."

Ah, Myles Porter. A sore subject.

"I did like him," I told her. "Until Olivia Miner stole him. Just like she stole Luke Lasky," I pointed out. "And just like she's going to steal Jeremy Ryan, too, if I'm gone."

I didn't say this, but I was pretty sure that naturally tan, naturally terrible Olivia Miner was put on this planet for no reason *but* to steal boys from me.

"Oh, Sam." My mom rolled her eyes then. "I really can't keep up with your crushes. And I'm definitely not going to work our vacations around them."

"I think going to the beach sounds sweet, Mom!" Josh chimed in.

I shot him exactly the kind of who-asked-you glare that he deserved. "Of course you do," I snapped. Karen's son, Brian, was the same age as him, after all. But her other kids, Kiki and Emery, were still practically babies. "You'll have Brian," I told Josh. "But who am *I* going to hang out with? There won't be anyone there my age at all." Then I pointed to the TV on the counter by the table. "Have you talked with Dad about this?" I asked, turning back to my mom.

"Of course I have," she said. She nodded toward my dad, who was currently on the screen and pointing to a big rain cloud over Pennsylvania. "You know how much your dad loves the beach — and Karen and Jay. Unfortunately, he'll have to stay home and work a lot of the time. But he should be able to come down and meet us for part of the time."

My dad is a weatherman on Channel 3: Mack Macintosh. (And no, "Mack" is not his real name.

It's Marvin. But that's just between us.) My mom used to be his producer, but now she makes commercials for the cable company occasionally. She's even let me be in some. I was most recently seen scarfing food in the background of a commercial for Tico's Tacos, and dropping a bowling ball on my toe in one for Central Jersey Lanes. (No joke — she kept that in there. She thought I was trying to be funny. Right, Mom.)

My mom went on, "And don't worry, honey — there *will* be kids your age. Karen says the house is so big, she's invited Jackie and her family, too." I swear she was smiling so hard, it looked like her teeth might pop out of her head. "Won't that be great?"

Great? I wasn't about to go that far. But better . . .

Jackie was my mother's *other* roommate from college — and she was a lot easier to take. (She wears normal shoes, for one thing.) I hadn't seen her or her family for a long time — maybe four years — but I'd never forget what a great time I had with her daughter, Juliette. I was seven, and Juliette was eleven. And the minute we got together, we were like sisters! (There is absolutely, positively nothing in this whole world that I want more, by the way, than a sister . . . except maybe

10

for Jeremy Ryan to be my boyfriend.) We hung out together the whole weekend. Our parents even let us sleep in the same room. Juliette taught me how to do cat's cradle and make a French braid and speak pig Latin and do a handstand in the pool. We even had the same favorite number — eleven, her age and my soccer number!

Suddenly, two months at the beach — with Juliette! — didn't seem so bad after all. Especially since my other wish-they-were-sisters, Mina and Liza, were already going to be away. Sigh.

I did regret that I didn't have any more hair for Juliette to braid. I'd just had it all chopped off and mailed it to Locks of Love, for kids who don't have any hair of their own. I was totally psyched to do it as soon as I saw it on the news. I mean, I don't have the most gorgeous hair (it's pretty stringy and this color that a kind, generous person might call dirty blond) but it was better than nothing, right? Plus, I read somewhere that your hair grows thirty feet in your lifetime. So I figured if I started now, I could donate it maybe twenty more times!

The day after I saw the story, I had my mom take me to the place where she gets her hair cut. My mom has short hair, and even though it's starting to get gray, it still looks pretty good. So I figured her hair guy could make someone young like me look like a rock star. Right? Wrong. (Unless you're talking about a *male* rock star.) Mina and Liza both say I look great. But they're my best friends — they have to. If only I'd known I'd be spending the summer hanging out with Juliette, I might have waited until the end of August to cut all my hair off. (And then the ice-cream truck guy wouldn't have called me a boy in front of Jeremy Ryan on the way home from school. And I was wearing a barrette, too! That's why a boy's name like "Sam" was the last thing I needed to be called, thank you!)

Maybe Juliette would think my haircut was cool.

I closed my eyes and could practically see us together at the beach, talking about boys and makeup and clothes. It wasn't going to be like hanging out with Liza and Mina — nothing was. But close, I hoped!

"Okay, Mom," I said. "I'll go to Karen's beach house. But can we at least have ice cream for dessert?"

And now, just a few weeks later, school was over. I was officially twelve (and one year closer to the big thirteen!). And if the huge green bridge in front of us meant what I thought it did, we were almost at the beach. . . .

Chapter Two

My mom rolled down the windows, and that unmistakable beachy smell filled the car at once: salt, sand, and even a little coconut oil mixed in. I took a deep breath. I couldn't see the ocean yet — the dunes and tall beach grass blocked my view — but I knew it was out there, just past the sign that said WELCOME TO SALT ISLE. And I was suddenly filled with this jittery feeling. I couldn't wait to get to the house!

Then I had to gasp for breath. The air smelled nice and all. But it was hot out there!

My mom turned down the soundtrack to *South Pacific*. "Sam, call your dad, sweetie," she said, tossing her cell phone back to me. "Tell him we're almost there!"

"Sure," I sighed. "But call me Samantha, please, Mom."

She grinned and looked back at me in the rear-view mirror. "I keep forgetting, hon. I'm sorry."

I quickly called my dad's work number. It was just about three o'clock — two hours before he had to be on the air.

"Suzanne?" he answered, saying my mom's name since I was calling from her phone.

"No, Dad," I said. "It's me."

"Well, hey there, sunshine!" he said. "Where are you guys? Everything okay?"

"Yep. We're here. Almost. Mom said to call. We miss you."

"I miss you, too, sunshine. But you made good time! Hey, what's the temp?" he asked. (It doesn't take long for my dad to talk weather.)

I glanced at the gauge on the dash. "Ninety-one," I replied. Then I breathed deeply again. "But it feels like a hundred."

"Ooh, scorcher!" he said. "Well, get used to it. I'm looking at the air pressure, and it doesn't look like the heat's going anywhere for quite a while. And tell your mom to buy extra sunscreen. The UV index is only getting higher. Give her a big kiss for me, too, sunshine. And Joshie, too, of course."

I looked over at my brother, who was picking away at his nose. I had to swallow hard to keep the milk shake I'd had with lunch from coming up at the thought of kissing him. "Uh, sure, Dad. Of course." (Right.)

"Good. And, hey — save some fun for when I get there, okay?"

I grinned. "Okay, Dad. Love you."

I hung up and turned my attention back out the window. This beach road was a lot different from the ones in New Jersey that I was used to. Where were all the T-shirt shops and ice-cream stands? Where was the amusement park? And the arcade? All this place had was beach houses, as far as I could see.

"So, uh, where's the boardwalk?" I finally asked my mother.

"Oh, I don't think there is one, honey," she said.

"No boardwalk?" Where would Juliette and I hang out? "So what do kids *do* here?" I asked her.

"Well . . ." She shrugged. "I guess they go to the beach."

Every day? For eight weeks?

"Oh, look!" my mom went on. "You can also play putt-putt."

"Putt-what?" I echoed.

"Miniature golf. See." She pointed to a minia-ture lighthouse surrounded by various strips of green. She read the sign: "Lighthouse Putt-Putt. Looks like fun to me!"

I sighed. Thank goodness Juliette was going to be there, or this would be a very long eight weeks!

Finally, we turned off the main road. Before I knew it, we were driving toward a big house with a sign on the front that said ISLE BE BACK.

I totally loved it!

"Is that it?" I asked my mother. "Wow, it's pretty cool! I mean, it doesn't look quite as huge as you described it, but that roof deck looks like fun. And it has a pool! And a tennis court, too?" I almost hated to admit it, but this place was going to be awesome!

"Huh?" my mom said absentmindedly. "Tennis court? Pool? Oh no, hon. That's not it." She laughed. Then she drove right by the house and pointed to another one behind it. "There you go. The Drift Inn. That's us." She pulled up and turned off the car's engine.

"Whoa!" Josh cried. "Big one!" And he was right. Or he would have been, if he'd been talking about the ginormous mansion looming in front of us and not some three-pointer he'd just scored on his DS game. "Yes!" he added, pumping one fist in the air. "In your face!"

But back to the "beach house." I mean, I'd seen some big houses — Olivia Miner's came to mind — but this thing was out of control. Way bigger than the other house I'd been looking at. So big that there wasn't even *room* for a tennis court or pool around it. I'd assumed it was some kind of old hotel or school or something.

And by "old," I mean . . . a *total* mess.

We could start, for example, with the windows, which were caked in salt and basically impossible to see through.

Or we could talk about the shutters, which didn't open out, but were more like boards propped up by sticks. They were the heavy eyelids on a house that truly looked like it needed to be put to sleep.

Or we could talk about the gray, weathered shingles all over the outside — or maybe not, since half of them, at least, had blown away.

Or we could talk about the roller coaster of a covered porch that dipped and swayed all around the first floor.

17

Or maybe we should talk about the wobbly stilts keeping the huge house from sinking into the sand. I mean, I could totally see taking *one* step inside and having the whole house collapse on me.

Honestly, it looked more like a sunken battleship that had washed up onshore than something human beings should be living in. *They should change the weathered sign from Drift Inn to Cave Inn or Inn Big Trouble,* I thought.

That and, *I want to go home!*

And then Karen came outside.

"Hey, y'all!" she yelled, jogging down the front steps and waving like crazy. She had on a bathing suit and some kind of tie-dyed sarong. But at least she wasn't wearing any crazy shoes. That was a plus.

My mom jumped out of the car and ran up to hug her — which always looks funny to me, since Karen's so teeny and my mom is six feet tall.

"I thought y'all would never get here!" Karen cried. She and my mom pulled back and looked at each other, then squealed and hugged again. "We're gonna have so much fun!" Karen went on. "Now, let me see those adorable children of yours! It's been too long."

My mom turned back to the car, shielding her

eyes from the sun, and hollered for us. "Guys, come on. What are you waiting for?"

Uh, I'm waiting for Jeremy Ryan to ride up on a big white horse and carry me away, I wanted to answer. But I didn't. What was the point? Instead, I slowly opened my door.

"Come on," I told Josh.

"No way," he said, thumbs frantically tapping away at his DS. "I still have two minutes left in the period."

I sighed and climbed out alone.

"Sam?" cried Karen immediately. "Is that really you?" She trotted over and grabbed me in a hug that was surprisingly hard for such a small person. *Great,* I thought. *Now I'm going to smell like her weird perfume.*

"Hi," I mumbled, trying to smile. And as soon as she was done hugging, I added, "You can call me Samantha now. Everyone does."

"Samantha!" said Karen. "Oh, my goodness, you've grown up since last fall! I do declare you're taller than I am now! And that adorable haircut! Why, Suzanne —" She turned to my mom. "She's just the spittin' *image* of you!"

I must have looked a little upset at that idea, since my mom assured me, "She's exaggerating. Don't worry. And yes," she said to Karen, "her hair does look good, doesn't it?" She smiled at me proudly. "You know why she cut it? For Locks of Love."

"No, you did not!" Karen hugged me again, and I couldn't help coughing. *Ugh!* All that yoga had made her pretty strong. "If that's not the sweetest thing I've ever heard! I swear, I would do that in a second with my hair," she said, putting her hand up to the strawberry blond curls that surrounded her freckled face, "if my hair ever decided to grow down instead of out. Oh, well." She laughed. "Hey! What are we doin' standin' out here in the sun? Samantha, honey, you must be boilin' in those clothes. Shall we go inside?"

I looked down at my black tights and fingerless gloves, then up at the house, and kind of shrugged.

"Yeah, it's not much, is it?" Karen said with a nod. "I'm so sorry. I'd hoped to have it fixed up more before y'all got here." She heaved a sigh. "But it's a lot more work than I'd expected. Jay says we should change its name from Drift Inn to Inn Over Our Heads."

Good one, Jay, I thought.

"You know," Karen went on, "this place used to be a hotel." (Yes! I was right!) "My granddaddy actually won it in a poker game when he came back from World War Two."

"So how'd *you* get it?" I asked.

Karen shrugged. "The only heir left," she said. Then she rolled her eyes. "Well . . . actually, the only one willing to take it on."

I nodded. I wasn't surprised.

"Jay and I know we could fix it up and rent it out," Karen explained. "But before we decide to invest the money and keep it for good, we thought we'd spend a summer here and make sure we really want it. Luckily, an engineer told us it's sound. She said it would take at least a category-five hurricane to knock this old place down."

Yeah, I thought, *that or a category-one sneeze.*

"Well, I love it!" my mom declared.

I had to look at her and frown. I couldn't help it.

"It's fantastic!" my mom went on, ignoring my glare. "And I know Marvin's going to love it, too."

"Well, if you like it now," said Karen, "just wait till you see the inside!"

My mom turned back to the car. "Hey, Josh! Let's go!" she yelled. "Turn off that game and get out here *now!*"

At last, Josh climbed out, said hello to Karen,

and the three of us followed her up the old steps into the house.

"It reeks," said Josh.

"Mildew," Karen explained, before my mom could snap at Josh for being rude. "What can you do?" She shrugged. "It's the beach!"

Well, you could toss out all these moldy chairs and sofas, I thought as I looked around a big room filled with dusty, faded furniture. At one time, I guessed, it had all been green and blue. Now it was all pale and grayish — like construction paper when you leave it in the sun. And you could turn on some air-conditioning, too, since it was at least a hundred degrees hotter inside than out. Oh, and you could also cover your nose, which was exactly what I did with the black, skull-patterned scarf Liza had given me for my birthday.

"It is a little musty, isn't it?" said Karen.

"And hot," I groaned.

"Sam!" my mom said, giving me a look.

"Well, we don't have any air-conditioning, I'm afraid," said Karen. "Takes a little gettin' used to. . . ."

"No air-conditioning?" I couldn't help gasping. "None at all?"

"No, darlin'. Sorry," Karen replied. "But we'll get these ceiling fans workin' soon — don't you worry."

I looked up at the fan above us. It had two blades instead of four. It looked like Juliette and I would be hanging out on the beach, no matter what!

"So where's Brian?" Josh piped up.

"Down at the beach with Jay and the girls," Karen said.

"Josh, why don't you bring in your bag and put on your bathing sui — " my mother began.

But she was wasting breath on him, as usual. By then, Josh was long gone.

My mom rolled her eyes. "Do you want to go, too?" she asked me.

I shrugged. I could have used the fresh air, I guessed. But something made me want to see more of the disastrous house. So I stayed with my mom and Karen — and tried to breathe through my mouth as much as I could.

"So this is one of the sitting rooms," Karen said as she led us to a large room just off the front hall. "My granddaddy called it the Fish Room. I do believe he caught every one."

I looked around at the *hundreds* of stuffed fish lining the walls. There were some especially big ones with long, pointy noses, but most were more normal looking. They were all totally gross.

Then we moved on to the Buoy Room, which was completely decorated with buoys and big round life preservers. Somehow, someone had even managed to make furniture out of them. Then there was other stuff made out of thick, white rope — chairs, a sofa, and even a rope table with a slightly cracked, dust-covered piece of glass on top.

"And this is the dining room, or the Shell Room, as my grandmama called it," explained Karen, moving through a doorway.

"Look at that chandelier!" My mom gasped.

It was made — surprise! — completely out of shells.

So, basically, not only had this house absorbed every watt of heat from the sun; it had also let the ocean roll in and throw up absolutely everywhere.

The kitchen was a little more normal. In fact, it was actually cool. Or maybe I should say "not bad looking," since it was by no means a comfortable temperature. But it was about twice the size of our kitchen at home, and all the appliances were super-old — like, from a black-and-white TV show.

"Does this really work?" I asked Karen, pointing to the stove.

"Good question." She bit her lip. "Haven't got to it yet, but we're working on it. Don't worry, though. Jay's a whiz with raw food!"

"Raw food?" I said. "Like cereal?"

"No, darlin'." Karen shook her head and grinned. "Cereal's cooked before you get it. *Raw* food never gets any heat at all. It's surprisingly tasty . . . and handy when the stove's not workin'."

So's the microwave, I thought. But as I looked around, I didn't see one.

"Relax," Karen said. I think she noticed the look of pure panic that crossed my face. "We have a grill, too."

I sighed a little, unzipped my hoodie, and fanned it in and out. "Do you, um, have anything to eat right now?" I asked hopefully. My insides were suddenly rumbling, and I was really, really hoping there might be Fudgsicles in the big white "icebox."

Karen clapped her hands. "Oh, of course, darlin'. Where are my manners? I can't believe I haven't offered y'all any refreshment after such a long trip. How 'bout a nice, cold glass of sun tea, and some fresh figs?"

"Mmm," said my mom. "That sounds great."

Tea and figs? Oh no. I didn't think so.

"Samantha?" Karen said.

I couldn't help it. "Um, no thank you. Do you have Popsicles, by any chance?" I asked.

Karen shook her head. "Sorry, hon. I don't." She turned to my mom. "Haven't kept sugar in the house since Brian was two. That and wheat. It makes a big difference in his behavior."

No sugar? No wheat? I thought. *What else is there to eat?*

"I'll bet there are some frozen bananas in the icebox. How 'bout one of those?" Karen asked.

I probably shrugged.

I could see my mom giving me the stink eye.

"I know. How 'bout some watermelon?" said Karen.

My stomach rumbled happily. "Yes, please." Bingo!

"Great!" said Karen. "But let's cut it outside, shall we? One drop of food in this kitchen," she added, "and I'm afraid the ants literally come marching in, two by two."

Ants? I looked down at the floor and raised up onto the tippy-toes of my pink boots.

Great.

*   *   *

The back porch was shady, at least, and a relief from the inside of the house. (Who needs a working oven when you can bake pizzas in the dining room?) Plus, the bright-colored towels and bathing suits draped along the porch railing gave it a way more cheerful look — like an old bike dressed up with streamers and those plastic things on the spokes. It wasn't easy to find a place to put down a whole watermelon, though. The porch leaned so much, it took all three of us to keep the big green beast from rolling away.

As soon as things were under control and Karen starting cutting, I turned and looked out over the dunes behind the house. The sea grass growing on them stood up straight and tall, and since there was no breeze, it blocked most of the view of the beach below. Still, I could hear people calling and splashing, and I could see the blue-green Atlantic in the distance drifting out to meet the sky. As the sweet smell of watermelon filled my nose, I closed my eyes and thought for the first time, *Okay,* this *is summer vacation. . . .*

Arf, arf, arf!

I opened my eyes and looked up, surprised.

"Did you get a puppy?" my mom asked Karen.

She laughed. "Puppy? Oh no. That's just Emery. Jay must be bringing the girls up to see you."

Sure enough, a minute later Karen's spaniel-size, dark-haired three-year-old came bounding up over the dunes. Barking loudly, she trotted down the wooden walkway toward the porch on her hands and knees.

"Be careful, sugar pie," said Karen. "We don't want to find another splinter in that sweet little paw."

"Arf, arf," the little girl replied.

Karen stopped cutting the watermelon for a moment, and glanced up at me and my mom. "She thinks she's a dog, bless her heart, ever since I taught her the downward dog position in yoga. We do yoga out here on the porch in the mornings." She grinned. "Anyway, Emery's imagination just ran with it, I guess."

"Heel, Emery," a high voice called from the porch steps. Kiki clomped up the stairs into view. She was five, short, skinny, and completely covered in freckles and sand.

"Bad girl, Emery," said Kiki sternly. "Go sit in the corner."

Emery knitted her thin, dark brows together and plopped down, panting, at her mother's feet.

"Now, Kiki, be a good master," said Karen. "And

mind your manners. You have guests. Look, it's Samantha!"

Kiki cocked her head and looked me over. "Where's *Sam*?" she said.

"This *is* Sam," said Karen, chuckling. "She just cut her hair." Karen turned to me and smiled. "Kiki's been so excited to see you, Samantha, darlin'. We've been looking at pictures from last fall," she explained. "Too bad we didn't have a new one with you lookin' so chic!"

Kiki looked me over. "You look different," she said.

I adjusted the ruffles on my tutu skirt. "Thanks," I said.

She grinned and reached for my sleeve with her sandy hand. "You're welcome! Hey, do you wanna play Polly Pocket?"

"Uh . . ." I muttered, firing another look at my mom. *I'd rather do yoga with Karen,* I thought.

"Kiki, darlin'," said Karen, "give Samantha a second. She just got here. I'm sure she'll want to play with you later." (*You're sure?* I thought.) "But right now, it's time for watermelon. Who wants some?"

"I do!" called Jay as he reached the porch. He wore a loose white shirt, and a floppy straw hat to cover his bald spot. He gave my mom a hug.

"Welcome to our humble abode, m'lady!" he said. (Which is exactly how he always talks, I'm afraid.)

Then he turned to me. "And greetings to you, Sam! I like your new style — very Emo!" he declared with two thumbs up.

I tried not to roll my eyes — even though everyone knows that Emos wear Chuck Taylors and straight-leg pants, not combat boots and tutus. "Actually, it's Goth," I said very patiently. (He probably would have known that if my mom just let me wear black eyeliner and dye my hair pink. But she says no chance until I'm in high school. Oh, well.)

"So, hon, where are the boys?" Karen asked, handing him a slice of melon. The pink juice left a trail of sticky drips across the porch.

"They're chasing seagulls and eating fiddler crabs — raw," Kiki said, before her dad could answer.

Ew!

"Don't worry," Jay said. "They're fine. They should be up soon."

Karen handed me another slice of watermelon and I took a big, slurpy bite. *Mmm*. It wasn't *Fudgsicle* good . . . but it was icy-cold and sweet. It definitely did the trick.

Karen clicked her tongue. "Well, they'd better

hurry if they want some watermelon," she said, placing a slice on a napkin and putting it on the deck in front of Emery.

"Arf, arf," Emery barked, bending forward to dig in. She was pretty good at eating with no hands, I had to admit.

Kiki, on the other hand, was already covered in juice and fuchsia watermelon bits. "Okay, I'm done," she said, handing a half-eaten slice back to her mother. Then she grabbed my arm with her two sticky hands. "What do you like better?" she asked. "Polly Pocket or Littlest Pet Shop? I have both!"

Karen reached out and stroked Kiki's curly red hair. "Poor Kiki," she told my mom. "She gets so tired of playing puppy all the time with a three-year-old. . . ."

Poor *Kiki*? How about poor me? I was twelve and a *week* already! I hadn't come to the beach to play with a five-year-old!

I turned to my mom for some support, but I was saved by the car horn.

Jay dabbed at his chin with a towel. "Jackie's carriage has arrived, I do believe!" he said.

I would have groaned, but I was suddenly too happy. Juliette was here — now summer vacation could *really* begin!

Chapter Three

I ran around (and up and down) the wobbly porch to the front of the house. Juliette's mom, Jackie, was the first to get out of the car. She had on a bright pink-and-orange sundress, and her blond hair was held back with a matching scarf. She looked just like a mom from a TV show — the kind where everyone lives in a neat, perfect house and eats big weekend breakfasts, like pancakes, even on school days. After my mom's reunion a few years back, I remembered thinking how great it would be to live with her and *really* be sisters with Juliette. Sure, I'd miss my parents and my friends — but besides that, it would be awesome!

Of course, then my parents would be stuck

alone with just Josh, and that would be totally unfair to them.

I stood on the steps and watched Jackie lift her sunglasses to her forehead. "Sam? Is that you?" she said.

Oh, brother. Not again.

"It's *Samantha* now . . . but yes. Hi!" I said, waving.

Just then, my mom and Karen came running around, and the next thing I knew they were all hugging one another and squealing and jumping and even, yes, *crying*. OMG!

Jay came up behind me. "Girls will be girls." He chuckled. "Am I right, Lady Samantha?"

Lady Samantha? "Uh, yeah . . ." I said, nodding — agreeing, and at the same time marveling how anyone could be so weird.

Then he loped down the steps and joined the meet and greet in the driveway. *Jay will be Jay,* I thought, along with *Moms are really weird and embarrassing sometimes*. I knew they hadn't all been together like this in years. But *still*. And besides, all this "I've missed you so much!" and "It's so good to see you!" and "We're going to have so much fun!" was making me miss my own BFFs. A lot.

Get out here already, Juliette! I thought. I looked down at my skirt and my tights and my bright pink combat boots and my hoodie . . . which was now covered with watermelon juice. (Oops.) Was it too much? Should I have worn my black boots instead? Or maybe my plaid leggings and that supercute purple vest?

My mom looked up and waved at me. "Come down and say hi, Sam . . ."

I waited.

". . . antha!" she added.

I waved back and very coolly (in case Juliette was watching) walked down from the porch.

Juliette still hadn't come out of the car, but Jackie greeted me with open arms.

"*Samantha!* I love your hair!" she exclaimed. "And you've gotten so tall! You look just like your mom!" She hugged me tight, and I couldn't help smiling.

"Uh . . . thanks," I said.

I had to remind myself that my mom's old friends knew her back when she was young and surprisingly pretty. So when they said that I looked like her, it really wasn't so bad.

"Don't tell me you're just eleven," Jackie said.

"No, actually, I'm *twelve*," I said. "My birthday was last week."

"Speaking of birthdays," Jay piped up, "if I remember correctly, Dave must have just had his. Where art thy better half, anyway?" he asked Jackie.

I didn't listen to the response, because I was too busy watching the passenger-side door of Jackie's car slowly open, instead. And out stepped not Juliette's dad, Dave, but Juliette herself!

Or maybe I should say she *glided* out — like a movie star arriving at the red carpet, or an American Idol at their hometown parade. Only way cooler.

Juliette had her blond hair up in a high pony-tail, but it was soft and loose in front. And she was wearing three layered tank tops, plus these cute, longish surf shorts and awesome green-checkered Vans. (Too bad Vans weren't Goth.) Plus, I could tell that she had on makeup — but in a way I knew even my mom would think looked good.

Instantly, any worries I'd had about the sum-mer — about missing my friends or losing out on my shot at true love with Jeremy Ryan — all melted away. (Kind of like me in that beach house.) With Juliette around, my summer was going to be awesome!

I watched as Juliette walked around to the trunk, pulled out a bag, and slung it over her shoulder. She marched right past me, up to her mother. "I need to go to my room and make some calls," she announced stiffly. She looked at Karen. "Hi. Thanks for having us. Where should I go?"

"Oh, go right inside, darlin', and up the stairs," Karen replied. She gave Juliette a little hug. "And then just pick any old room you like. There are plenty."

"*Nuestro casa es su casa*," said Jay.

(I take Mandarin, not Spanish, but I think that means something like "make yourself at home.")

"Thanks," Juliette said softly.

I grinned, raised my hand, and began to say, "Hi! I'll go with you!" But before I could even open my mouth, Juliette had walked up the steps and into the house. Alone.

As the screen door slammed shut, I stood there speechless. And yes, embarrassed. Ouch.

I guess I should have worn the leggings, I immediately thought. *Or done something cuter with my hair?* Then it hit me like a lightning bolt — my hair. Of course!

I felt it with my hands. Juliette hadn't recognized me!

The last time Juliette had seen me, I was a little girl with long hair. She'd probably looked around when she got out of the car, and assumed that I was someone she didn't know!

I was about to follow her and tell her, when Kiki ran up and tugged at my sleeve. Emery crawled along behind her.

"Are you ready to play now?" Kiki asked me.

"Arf, arf, arf!" Emery sat up on her haunches and pawed at my leg.

"Bad dog, Emery. Down!" Kiki said.

I stepped back toward the house. "Sorry, guys," I said, trying to make it clear that I was much too old for *playing*. "I have calls to make, too."

"You do?" my mom asked.

I nodded. I hadn't talked to Mina or Liza, and I wondered how their trips were going so far. Even more than that, though, I wanted to head inside and find Juliette.

"Oh, Samantha, why don't you go up and pick out a room, too?" said Karen.

"Can't she sleep with me?" asked Kiki.

"No, sugar pie." Karen smiled at me. "Samantha gets her own room." She walked up and picked Kiki up and kissed her on the cheek. "Besides, you have a roommate already. Remember? Emery."

"But Emery howls at night." Kiki frowned at her sister, then turned to me. "And she's not really a dog either," she whispered.

I tried not to giggle. "I had a feeling," I said, pulling my bag out of our car and heading up the porch steps.

Inside the house, I tried to hold my breath. But I gave up on that before long, and concentrated on dragging my bag up the creaky, old stairs instead. (Do they really have to make combat boots so heavy?)

Upstairs, I discovered a seemingly endless hallway of bedrooms, numbered 1 to 16. Most of the doors were open, and the rooms sat musty and empty. There was one littered with Polly Pockets and other random toys that I figured was Emery and Kiki's. And I could tell which room was Brian's without even looking — because it smelled exactly like dirty boy feet.

Only one door was closed: number 11. Bingo! That had to be Juliette's.

I raised my hand and was just about to knock, when I heard her talking. She *was* on the phone, and as an almost-teenager I knew that interrupting phone calls was not cool. I'd wait, I decided. And in the meantime, I'd claim my own room.

It was a tough call. I wanted to be right next to Juliette, but the way the rooms were numbered, that meant room number 9 or number 13. I wasn't crazy about either one. 9 was so three years ago.

(And besides, the room had a GIANT spider on the ceiling, right above the bed.) But 13 was so . . . well, jinxed, cursed, *doomed*. It didn't seem very conducive to sleeping, or even staying alive. But it did have this awesome green wallpaper with starfish all over it — and a matching bedspread, too. And it did have a big, sagging bookshelf filled with paperbacks with great titles like, *And Then There Were None* and *Death on the Nile* and *Murder on the Orient Express*. Plus, on the table by the bed was a lamp made out of a conch shell with a hula girl attached. Her grass skirt actually wiggled if you pushed it.

And no spiders! (At least none that I could spot.)

Of course, there was always room number 10, right across the hall from Juliette's room. But ten was Olivia Miner's soccer number, so in a way, that was even more cursed than thirteen.

Room 13 it was. The more I thought about it, the more fitting it seemed — teen *and* Goth!

So I went in and dropped my bag on the floor, then sat on the bed and pulled out my phone. *Should I call Mina and Liza?* I wondered. *Or just text them?*

Only then did I realize that I wasn't going to do either. My phone was completely dead.

Great. I searched through my bag, tossing my clothes around the room. I dug through every pocket, pulled out every article of clothing, even turned my bag upside down and shook it out. But there was no denying it — I'd forgotten my charger. Argh.

I sighed and picked up the framed photo that had fallen out on the bed with the rest of my stuff. My mom had taken it of me, Mina, and Liza at the "See Ya Soon" party we had at my house, on my birthday, before we all left. There was Mina, looking all artsy and cool, and Liza making a face, and me with a smile that said plainly: "Help! I ate too much cake!"

Oh! I was *dying* to know what they were doing right now! I propped the photo up next to the hula girl lamp, then I tried to think. Could I use my mom's charger? Or could Juliette, maybe, have the same phone as me? I could ask her! And even if she didn't have a charger for me to use, it was a way to politely interrupt and tell her who I was!

I walked out of my room and up to her door, and knocked very softly.

Nobody answered. I guessed she was done talking. So I took a deep breath and knocked again.

After another minute, the door swung open. Juliette stood there with the same look on her face that my mom gets when she answers "junk-mail phone calls" (as she calls them) during dinner.

"Hi! It's me," I said. "Samantha!"

Juliette looked at me with a blank expression that still didn't seem to know me — and didn't seem to want to either.

"Sam," I went on, trying to light a spark of recognition. "You know, Suzanne's daughter? I don't go by that name anymore, though. Of course, my mom keeps forgetting and still calls me Sam all the time, which is totally weird, since she's the one that gave me the name Samantha in the first place. So, how do you like your room? I'm right next door, in room thirteen. You don't think that's unlucky, do you? I mean, spending the summer cooped up here with all these younger kids is unlucky enough, right? Plus, Karen says there's no air-conditioning. Can you believe it? She gave us a whole tour. If you want, I can show *you* around whenever. . . ."

I finally paused to take a breath. (Sometimes I can get a little rambly.)

And that was when Juliette slammed the door.

Chapter Four

So my first day of vacation didn't go exactly as planned. Or anything like I'd planned, really. The whole summer-sister thing I'd been dreaming about burst like a bubble and fizzled away somehow. (And I couldn't even talk to Mina or Liza about it on my dead phone!)

I wondered if Juliette had just had a miserable trip or something. Or maybe she'd had some horrible, fabulous teenage boyfriend drama (which she'd hopefully talk to me about later)! Who knew? So I sucked it up and decided to give her some space. We had the whole rest of the summer to talk about boys and hang out, after all.

Or maybe not.

Because as the rest of the summer progressed, things with Juliette didn't get any better. In fact, here's how the first week of my "vacation" went:

- Get woken up at the crack of dawn by Kiki and Emery — one pouncing on my bed, the other barking loudly.
- Rinse off all the tiny ants that crawled onto my toothbrush from the sink, and try not to gag as I brush my teeth.
- Get dragged down to the porch for dog-friendly yoga with Kiki and Emery and — as my mom and her friends like to call themselves — the "girls."
- Choke down a bowl of yogurt and something called muesli, which tastes a lot like hamster food. (I'm just guessing.)
- Head out to the beach, since by nine A.M. the Drift Inn was way too hot to hang out in. (Did I mention that there was no Internet? Or TV? There was one phone at the bottom of the front stairs. But it was big and heavy and the handset was connected by a thick, twisty cord, and you had to dial by sticking your finger in a hole and turning a wheel and then talk in front of anyone who happened to be passing by. Very weird.)

Somehow, Juliette managed to sleep in every day until noon. I guess she was lucky enough to have a working fan in her room. Mine was so noisy and wobbly, I was afraid it would fly off and chop me to bits while I was sleeping. So I kept it off, and silently roasted to medium rare every night.

One night, we did at least go play miniature golf (or "putt-putt," as everyone else liked to call it). And at first I thought, *Hooray! A chance to hang out with Juliette for eighteen holes.* But wouldn't you know it, Juliette decided to stay home. I had no idea what could have made her want to sit around the steamy hot house alone, and miss out on something so fun. But I figured I'd still have a good time.

I figured wrong.

First of all, we didn't go to the miniature golf course I wanted to try — the one with the volcano with real fire in the middle. Instead, we went to the one Josh and Brian voted for, with the fifty-foot-tall wooden pirate and the annoying real parrot that squawked constantly. And secondly, I got stuck on Josh and Brian's team, which meant there was no use keeping track of my score, because they "accidentally" whacked my ball into every waterfall, sand trap, or pool we came across.

Why do people keep score in miniature golf, anyway? It's just a game, after all. Who cares if it takes twelve strokes to get through a treasure chest? Or sixteen to get around a bubbling pit with a sign reading DANGER! QUICK SAND! Seriously.

In the end, I was actually glad to get home.

The beach was no picnic either, with both Josh and Brian around. I can handle one Josh, no problem. But multiply him and it starts to get iffy. I had to be on constant alert. Let down my guard for one minute, and the next thing I knew there'd be one twerp pinning my arms behind my back while another dumped a bucketful of seaweed in my hair. (Or worse.)

This beach wasn't like the Jersey shore beaches I was used to either. Not only was there no boardwalk, no cheesy gift shops, no Skee-Ball huts, and no stands serving hot, greasy fries and giant cones of frozen custard — there was no *nothing*. Not even a guy walking around selling Popsicles from a cooler. Nothing but sand and water, and adults who had no business prancing around in bathing suits, and packs of kids in soggy swim diapers. Fun? Nope.

I couldn't even lie on a towel by myself and read *Appointment with Death* or retake a *Tiger Beat* quiz. Because as soon as I did, Emery would appear, ready to dig a hole with her little "paws." Or Kiki would swoop in, begging to bury me in the sand. Eventually, I would take off my boots and my new Zombie Girl T-shirt, and I'd dive into the water in last year's old tankini. (Unfortunately, the one my mom had ordered for me this year had a big sea horse on it and was way too babyish for a twelve-year-old to wear.) Diving was the *only* way to go into the water, as far as I was concerned. No tiptoeing in up to your waist and going, "Ooh! It's cold!" But I never stayed in for very long. The waves were kind of boring, and I didn't have a float to use.

Plus, Josh and Brian would almost always swim up and pretend to be sharks.

The only mildly redeemable thing about the whole beach scene was the lifeguards. Especially the one with a thick, white, braided rope bracelet and wavy, sun-streaked brown hair. How did he compare to Jeremy Ryan?

All I can say is, Jeremy *who*?

I actually first noticed the lifeguard when he whistled at my brother to move his skimboard after Josh knocked down an old lady. The lifeguard stand was right near our beach house, and this was not Josh's first whistle. It probably wasn't even the first from this lifeguard, but I knew for

46

sure it was the first in front of me. I would have remembered him.

He stood up and motioned broadly for Josh and Brian to move down the shore. "No skimboards inside the flags!" he shouted. "I've told you guys before!"

Of course, Josh and Brian acted like they didn't hear him. Then they laughed, and Josh did his usual "Who, me?" shrug as the guard whistled again.

"Yes, you!" The lifeguard nodded. "Now, move it!" he called.

My hero! I thought.

I ducked my head to make it clear — hopefully — that I didn't know them. But I couldn't help looking back up at the lifeguard after a minute.

I wondered what color his eyes were beneath those dark sunglasses.

And I wondered where he learned to twirl his whistle around his finger so fast.

But I didn't have time to wonder much more before Kiki came running over.

"There you are! Can I bury you now? Please?" she asked.

I sighed. "Okay. But just one more time. That's all."

*　　*　　*

As it turns out, there is no such thing as doing something "just one more time" with a five-year-old. Nope. Not possible.

After Kiki buried me and I climbed out, she cried, "That was too easy! Let me do it again. *Please?*"

"Sorry," I told her, shrugging. "Remember? We had a deal."

Then her chin got all trembly.

"Oh, all right," I said. I probably couldn't get any more sandy than I already was, anyway. "But this time, how about you make me a mermaid tail?"

"How do you do that?" she asked.

"I'll show you," I said. I dug out a pit for Kiki to sit in, and covered up her legs with sand. Then I carved out a perfect fish tail, complete with layered shell scales, in the sand over them. (It's a little thing that Mina taught me when we were kids.)

"Cool!" Kiki cried, her eyes lighting up. "I look like a mermaid!"

I grinned. "Yes, you do! Now I'm going to read my book for a little while."

But before I could even sit down, I heard another little voice crying, "Oh, do me, too!" I turned to find not one, but about a dozen four-, five-, and six-year-olds flocking around me like greedy seagulls, begging for a turn.

It was not how I wanted to spend the next hour. But what choice did I have?

I had a pretty nice school of merfolk in the end, I had to admit.

Of course, there's this thing my mom sometimes says: "No good deed goes unpunished." And I never really got it before . . . but the beach taught me exactly what it meant: Look out when you do something nice, because it can totally come back to haunt you.

Take me, for example. If I had just blown off Kiki and her little friends that afternoon, it's very likely that I could have spent the whole rest of the summer in peace. But no, I entertained them. And what did I get? I got stuck being trailed by not just Kiki and Emery, but a whole crowd of rug rats every day after that! I couldn't lie out and get some sun, or go in the water, or even walk out of the house without something small and sandy jumping on me and holding on like a barnacle. That made it even harder to try to talk to Juliette . . . when she finally woke up and came outside in the afternoons.

"You know what I think, Samantha?" said Karen

one night, when we were all out on the porch eating dinner. (Did you know you could *grill* pizza? And if you very carefully picked off all the mushrooms and eggplant, it really wasn't that bad.)

"What?" I asked.

"Chicken butt!" yelled Josh from across the porch.

"Good one!" Brian said, belching.

"I think you'd make a mighty fine kids' yoga instructor," Karen told me. "You have such a way with them."

My mom squeezed my shoulder. "Doesn't she, though?"

I'd rather eat my weight in mushrooms, I thought.

Juliette's mom, Jackie, turned to her. "Why don't you get up a little earlier tomorrow and do some yoga with us, Juliette?" she said.

"It's a great way to ... take your mind off things, darlin'," Karen added sweetly.

I looked over at Juliette. "It's really not that bad," I said, shrugging.

Juliette sighed and shook her head. "I like to sleep," was all she said.

I guessed that was just what it was like to be sixteen: Sleep half the day; talk on the phone for the rest. I only wished I could sleep more.

Then the days might go much faster. But no such luck.

I tried a bunch of times in those first few weeks to sneak away from the little kids and find Juliette at the beach. I brought my iPod, some magazines, and of course my phone. (Yeah, it still had no charge, but you'd be surprised how satisfying a one-way conversation can be when you're trying to drive away a group of five-year-olds.) I tried to make small talk, which I'm usually good at . . . but with Juliette, it wasn't so easy.

"Check out that cloud," I said one afternoon. It was a particularly good day for cloud-spotting, which, if you ask me, is one of the best nothing-else-to-do things to do. "It looks just like a horse on a surfboard drinking a Slurpee, don't you think?"

Juliette raised her chin and scanned the sky behind her big sunglasses. "I don't see it," she said.

"Right there." I lay back and pointed straight up. I mean, it couldn't have been more obvious if I'd outlined it myself.

"Sorry." She shrugged.

"Oh, well." I didn't even ask her about the rabbit with a beard that I saw, too. It was changing into a duck-octopus thing by then, anyway.

Another time, I asked her if she wanted to read my *Tiger Beat*. I'd already pulled out the posters and hung them in my room at the Drift Inn. "There's a really good quiz this month," I said, "about which Jonas is right for you. Mine's Nick, of course! Though the first time I took the quiz, it was Kevin. But I must have done something wrong, because as far as I can tell, we don't have anything in common at all."

Juliette just shook her head. "No thanks," she replied.

I guessed she'd already read it. "So which Jonas do *you* like?" I asked. It was a pretty safe question, since everyone I knew liked at least one.

"Mmm, I don't know," she said. "I'm not really into them anymore."

"Not even Joe?" I said, stunned.

She just shook her head. I couldn't believe it!

"So what music *do* you listen to?" I asked her. She listed all these bands I'd never heard of. (Though I was dying to listen to them after that!) So that conversation unfortunately ended pretty fast.

Finally, one afternoon I got up the courage to ask Juliette the big question I'd been dying to ask.

"So . . . do you have a boyfriend?" I said.

I was sure this would be the icebreaker! She'd spill her guts, and I'd learn all about her fabulous teenage life, and we'd bond just like sisters — again. But all Juliette did was shake her head.

"Me neither," I said, trying not to sound too disappointed. "But I probably would if we'd stayed home this summer. There's this one boy — his name's Jeremy Ryan — and he's so cute." I pointed to the lifeguard with the rope bracelet and gold-tipped brown hair, sitting in the lifeguard chair. "Almost *that* cute," I said. "He's really good at twirling that whistle, don't you think?"

Juliette glanced up at the lifeguard. "He's not bad," she replied.

Not bad? Hmm. I could see why Juliette didn't have a boyfriend, if her standards were *that* high.

"Anyway," I went on, "I didn't even know I liked Jeremy Ryan until the last day of school when he wrote in my yearbook, 'Have a great summer. See ya around.' And I was like, yeah, I *will* see you around! But now that we're spending the whole summer in North Carolina, Jeremy Ryan's going to be seeing Olivia Miner around instead of me. And I don't even have his number to text him. Not that I could text him, anyway, since I don't have the charger for my phone. I can't text my best friends either, which is torture. You're so lucky to be able to use your phone," I told her, pausing to take a breath.

"I'm not that lucky," she said quietly. "But . . ." She looked at me with a slightly puzzled face. ". . . I thought you were just talking on your phone a little while ago?"

Whoops.

"Uh . . ." (Yes, I did feel like an idiot because, yes, I kind of was.) "Well . . . yeah . . . I mean, no . . ."

All I can say is thank goodness for Frisbees — specifically the big, hard orange one that came whizzing into the back of my head right then.

"Ouch!" I cried.

Of course, I knew it was my brother's. I didn't even have to check.

"Excuse me," I told Juliette. Then I picked up the Frisbee, ran to the water, and flung it out over the ocean as far as I could.

I wiped my hands in satisfaction. Two birds killed with one stone: awkward phone subject changed, and annoying Frisbee gotten rid of! The only thing was, when I got back to my towel, Juliette was lying on her stomach with her eyes tightly closed.

Operation Bond with Juliette part five — or six, or seven; I'd lost count — was another no-go.

Plus, Kiki and her friends had tracked me down, and soon I found myself building custommade sand castles for the rest of the afternoon . . .

or at least until the seagull pooped, no kidding, right on my head.

At the end of a week, though, I couldn't help it; I went to my mom to complain. I plopped down next to her beach chair, which was in its usual spot — close enough to the surf that the waves kept her feet cool, but not so close that her hair (horror of horrors!) would get wet. Karen and Jay had just gone into the ocean with Kiki and Emery, while Jackie had gone up to the house to see if Juliette was awake and ready for lunch.

"Mom," I said simply, "I am *so* bored. There's nothing to do here. We have to go home. There's no way I'm making it through a whole two months of this."

"But we've only been here a week," said my mom, flipping back the wide brim of her sun hat.

I nodded. "Exactly," I said. "And all I can think about are the weeks, and days, and hours, and *seconds* ahead."

"But Sam, I don't understand. You have a whole beach to play on."

"Play?" I rolled my eyes. "Mom, I'm twelve years old. I don't *play*. Or have you forgotten, like you keep forgetting to call me 'Samantha'?" I raised my eyebrows and gave her a look.

"Oh, I'm sorry, sweetie. I do keep forgetting." She smiled. "But if you're so bored, why not make some friends? You're always so good at doing that."

I gazed around. "Make what friends? There isn't a single kid my age here." I'd looked! I scanned the beach every day to try to find kids my age to hang out with. But there was absolutely no one over the age of ten or under the age of thirty. Except for Juliette — and, well, that wasn't working out at all like I'd planned.

"Well, don't give up. Keep trying," my mom said, rubbing my shoulder. "And in the meantime, how about we do something together?"

"Like what?" I asked. I liked the idea, but I tried not to look *too* cheered up until I heard what she had in mind.

"Didn't you want to get something for Liza and Mina? We could go shopping."

I smiled. Perfect! "Yeah." I shrugged. "That sounds pretty good."

I definitely did need to get something to send to Mina and Liza. After all, I'd been there a whole week already. It wasn't like me to wait so long!

Plus, I suddenly had another idea.

I thought of Juliette in her perfect bikini, with her stack of *Glamour* and *Elle* magazines; her iPod nano clipped to her perky ponytail; her fingernails and toenails, all painted a glossy ocean blue. Then I thought of myself running around in my Goth outfits, or worse, my green-flowered tankini; my worn, Magic-Markered fingernails; and the same old magazines I'd been reading since I was nine years old.

Of course Juliette didn't want to have anything to do with me!

A shopping trip was definitely in order.

Chapter Five

There were a bunch of things on my shopping list, including — drumroll, please — a real bikini. It was way too hot in the clothes I'd been wearing. And I had to admit, I was kind of looking forward to a change. I was starting to get tan . . . and it was kind of hard to keep the whole Goth thing up after that.

Plus, I had to find the perfect souvenirs for Mina and Liza. And there was one more very important thing that I needed badly. Something I was craving and couldn't live without. Sugar!

My mom made me wait until the next afternoon, but then she took me to a surf shop down the road that Karen said was good. Surprisingly, it was — and it was air-conditioned, too! It was *so* good, in fact, that I didn't know where to start looking. There were racks and racks of bathing suits. And just when I thought I'd seen them all, there were a few racks more. Finding a two-piece should not have been a problem.

Except that it totally was.

"You're looking at *bikinis*?" said my mom, looking stunned. "Are you sure?"

"Yes," I replied calmly.

I grabbed a dark green one and a light green one, just to prove that I was totally serious and not at all hesitant about the bikini thing. Then I put back the dark green one (it had weird buckles), and quickly reached for a plaid one that looked kind of nice.

But I wasn't so sure.

I put it back . . . then picked it up . . . then put it back . . . then picked it up again.

All my waffling was worth it, though, because suddenly I spotted another bikini that was just right! It was black, and covered with tiny purple and green skulls. A bikini *and* kind of Goth? Done!

"Found it!" I told my mother.

"Great," she said. She was browsing in the old-lady sizes. "You know, you've inspired me. I think I'll get one, too."

"Are you *sure*?" I asked her. She couldn't be serious, right?

"Why not?" she said. She held up the same green one with buckles that I'd rejected (only bigger). "What do you think?"

I knew she didn't want to hear my answer.

"Absolutely not," I told her anyway. "I'll meet you up front."

"Wait," she called. "Don't you want to try that suit on?"

"Nope," I said. Taking off all your clothes in a dressing room is way too much work. Besides, the suit was meant for me!

"Are you sure?" she asked. "I really think you should."

"Mom," I groaned.

What I wanted to do was find some flip-flops. I'd had enough of sand-filled boots, and enough of bare feet on sand so hot that it could melt into glass at any moment.

There were whole bins full of flip-flops on the other side of the store. I found the bin labeled SIZE SEVEN and began to check them out. I spotted some green ones right away, but then I saw a black pair. I held them up next to my new bathing suit. Perfect!

Maybe I could get both. Or even better, I could get both and mix them up . . . and send the other mismatched pair to Mina or Liza. Fun! I thought for a second and decided they'd be perfect for Liza. (Mina wasn't too crazy about black or green, after all.)

But Mina *was* crazy about purple — she had been forever — and there was the cutest pair of purple sunglasses on a rack near the front of the store. I picked them up and tried them on. Mina would love them, but they weren't exactly *me*.

Then I tried on another pair that was big and round. They were a lot like the sunglasses that Jackie and Juliette wore. I looked at myself in the tiny mirror built into the top of the rack. They covered up half of my face, at least. Awesome!

What else would be fun to send to Mina and Liza? I gazed around the store. A towel with a picture of a lighthouse on it? Boring. Shorts with the words SURF'S UP written across the back? Cute! I checked the price tag. Not *that* cute. (Though I did find a cute pair of surf shorts like Juliette's for myself.)

Maybe a T-shirt? There were lots to choose from, but only one that really worked. It had a hang ten sign in one corner on the front, and I'D RATHER BE SURFING IN SALT ISLE written across the back. Little did Mina and Liza know that they were much better off wherever they were at the moment, and that I was neither surfing, nor exactly happy. But the shirts came in cool colors, and they were fun.

I added them to the pile in my arms as I heard my mom's voice call across the store. "Sam?"

I didn't say anything. How else was she going to learn?

"Sa-*am*," she called out again. After a pause, she added, "Antha?"

Close enough.

"Over here." I waved to her.

"Oh! There you are. I didn't recognize you in those funny glasses. Ready to go?" my mom asked.

"I guess. . . ." I looked at my reflection in the mirror. The sunglasses were not funny at all! I walked over to the register and I laid out my finds on the counter. I had two things for both Mina and Liza — but was it enough?

Definitely not. Not when there was a whole rack of shell necklaces to choose from!

"Ooh!" I said, reaching for one with a tiny dolphin in the middle, and another with a tiny yin-yang sign made out of mother-of-pearl. "For Liza and Mina," I told my mom. "They'll love them, don't you think?"

"They're great," said my mom with a nod of approval. "Did you want to send some postcards, too?"

Postcards! I hated to admit it, but my mom had pretty good ideas sometimes.

I picked out two with pretty beach scenes on them. But since those were kind of boring (and since I can never fit all that I want to say onto just one card), I picked out two more that showed a guy lying on the sand with his head covered up, and another guy's head sticking out of the sand beneath his arm. It looked like the first guy's head had fallen off and he was holding it! I so had to try that on the beach with someone — even Kiki — sometime.

I put the postcards on the counter with everything else.

"You're sure you don't want to try on that suit, Samantha?" said my mother. She laid the questionable bikini she'd picked out for herself on the counter next to mine. "It's always a good idea, you know."

"Final sale," said the clerk cheerfully.

"I'm sure," I told my mom. "It's perfect for me. I know it."

As soon as we left the store, the heat outside took my breath away. I suddenly appreciated how much cooler it was by the ocean. I wasn't ready to go back to the house yet, though.

I grabbed my mom's hand and dragged her next door. "I. Need. Real. Food."

"I'm not sure saltwater taffy's actually 'real food,'" my mom said, reading the sign in the store window. "But after you."

We walked in, and the combination of cool air and the smell of sugar made me instantly think of heaven. I mean, that's how it has to be. I'll bet anything the angels all look like the lady in the pink apron behind the store counter, too.

"What can I get you today?" she said brightly.

There were goose bumps on my arms — and not just from the temperature. I stared at the case full of fudge and taffy. *How about everything?*

"I don't know," I said. Then I had to swallow, since my mouth had gotten drooly. "How about a box of taffy, and a pound of fudge."

"Taffy *and* fudge?" my mom said, raising her eyebrows.

I gave her one of those "pretty please" looks that Kiki always gave me.

"Okay," she sighed.

"Which kind, dear?" asked the woman.

"Um . . . rocky road, please."

"Doesn't that have nuts?" asked my mom. "Don't forget, Josh can't eat them."

I grinned and nodded to the woman. "Rocky road, definitely. Besides," I told my mom, "Josh and Brian are always together. It wouldn't be fair for Josh to have fudge if Brian can't eat sugar."

"Hmph," said my mom. She turned back to the counter. "We'll take a quarter pound of plain, too."

I'm glad I didn't wait until we got home to eat most of that fudge. After five minutes in the hot beach house, it was a puddle of molten goo. And I'd been planning to offer some to Juliette after dinner!

Oh, well. All in all, that was just a minor disaster, compared to the colossal bikini-debut disaster the next morning.

Okay, fine. Maybe I should have tried the bathing suit on at the store. Then maybe I would have realized that the top and bottom were both a little big. Then again, who knows? Maybe I would have felt like I did when I put the suit on in the morning. *Big deal, so it's roomy. It still makes me look more grown-up.*

Plus, at first I was much more concerned about my mom's new bikini than my own.

I could hardly believe it when we all went out to the beach and she actually had it on.

"You look fantastic, Suzanne!" said Karen and Jackie.

You look ridiculous! I thought.

"Mom, you need a cover-up," I dutifully informed her. She had children, after all.

But instead of listening to me, she smiled and went off for a walk.

I couldn't watch! I decided to go for a swim instead. . . . And that was when I learned this valuable lesson: When a bathing suit that's too big gets wet, it will try its best to fall off. In fact, this is probably a law of physics or something that they teach you one day in high school. And if they don't, they should.

Oh, and here's something else I learned, although it isn't that surprising: If you think your brother and his friend are acting totally immature about your wearing a bikini to begin with, just wait until it gets wet and your towel is about a thousand yards up the beach.

I was glad, at least, that the cute lifeguard was not on duty that morning. And that Juliette was still in the beach house, sleeping soundly away.

Thank goodness for man's best friend, Emery, who fetched my towel as soon as I asked her to!

Chapter Six

So what was the best part about my dad finally getting to the beach?

A) He brought my phone charger.
B) He brought my guitar.
C) I totally missed him.
D) All of the above.
E) All of the above except for A, which, not to be harsh, was totally lame! And I know he said he looked all over the house for the charger, but I find that a little hard to believe. . . .

Anyway, the correct answer is E. And I was happy, at least, to have my dad and my guitar around (even if I still couldn't play it). But of course, my dad had to bring news of the weather with him, too. That's just how he rolls.

"Can you believe it?" he said after he'd carried his bag in and gone on and on and *on* about how much different and more "summery" I looked. "There's already a tropical storm brewing in the Atlantic — this early in the summer!" He raised his eyebrows like he'd given us some juicy scoop — like Miley Cyrus and Nick Jonas had gotten back together or something. (Then again, in The Land of No TV or Internet, how would I have known?) "It's going to be a very interesting hurricane season this year, I predict," he went on gleefully.

"Indeed!" said Jay.

"That's the last thing we need," Karen groaned.

We were sitting on the porch, just outside the Fish Room — Jay and Karen, my mom and Jackie, plus Emery, Kiki, and me. Josh was out cutting kite strings or something with Brian, I was sure. And since it was still early, Juliette hadn't gotten up yet.

I had really, really hoped that my new look would show her that I, too, had grown up. That I wasn't a little kid, but almost a teenager — like her — and that we could hang out together. But she didn't seem any more interested in me than she had before. I hadn't given up on Juliette completely . . . but I was pretty close.

"But here's the good news," my dad continued. "The fishing should be excellent!"

Oh, good grief.

It didn't take long. I knew it was coming. Some dads like to hang out at the beach, and swim or read or play paddle ball on the sand for hours, like my uncle Stan. But my dad likes to fish. A lot. And he woke me up the very next morning — early! — with a fishing pole in his hand.

"Rise and shine, sunshine," he told me. "Eighty-three degrees, barometer holding steady, four-mile-per-hour winds blowing from the southwest, and the tide is high. You know what that means, don't you?"

"Time for you to get a life?" I groaned, closing my eyes again.

"Very funny," he said. "No. It means it's fishing time!"

"I don't think so, Dad," I told him. If I'd had a sheet on me, I would have pulled it over my head. But it was so hot in my room, even at night, that I slept on top of the covers. I rolled over and tried to find a cooler spot on my pillow, instead.

"It'll be fun," my dad said.

"Is Josh going?" I asked.

"Of course!" he said cheerfully.

"Then it will *not* be fun."

"Oh, come on," he said. "Don't you remember how great it was last time we went?"

"No," I grunted. What I *did* remember was going to some lake and Josh slipping a half-dead fish down the back of my shirt. Oh, and the smell! The memory nearly made me gag right there in my own bed.

I don't even like to eat fish, never mind deal with them when they're alive.

"Well, I want you to come," my dad told me. "It would mean a lot to me."

That's just playing dirty, if you ask me.

"Okay." I sat up slowly and felt the top of my head. Ugh. The sun and salt were doing terrible, *terrible* things to my hair. "But you're buying me ice cream," I told him and smiled.

"Done." My dad grinned. He knew he was getting a good deal. "Meet you by the car in ten minutes," he said.

"Dad," I groaned. Couldn't he see I needed a shower?

"Okay. Fifteen."

I took a cool shower, then put on some shorts

and a green-striped halter tank. (There was no way Josh was slipping a floppy old fish down the back of that.) Then I made my way down the back stairs, which led straight into the kitchen. The house was pretty quiet. I don't think the morning yoga had even started on the back porch yet. I grabbed a plum out of the fruit bowl on the counter, then found my flip-flops in the Buoy Room and went outside.

My dad was standing by the car with Josh. But they weren't the only ones waiting for me. Jay and Brian were there, too. Great. I should have known.

"Mornin', m'lady," said Jay, opening the back door of his blue Prius. "Your carriage awaits!"

"I call shotgun!" Brian yelled.

"No, me!" cried Josh.

It was too early for this.

"You're both riding in the back," said my dad. "Let's go. The fish aren't going to catch themselves, you know."

Jay chuckled as he climbed into the driver's seat. "If only they could!"

I slid in behind him, while Josh and Brian rock-paper-scissored for the privilege of *not* sitting next to me.

I leaned forward in my seat. "By the way, Dad, you owe me a double scoop," I said.

"Who invented fishing, anyway?" I asked my dad about five minutes later, when we pulled up in front of the pier. "I mean, really, what's the point?"

"The point, my dear, is to catch fish," he said. "It's a sport."

Sport? Uh, I didn't think so. Fishing was standing around with a worm on a stick, waiting for a slimy old fish to choke itself on a little hook.

I made a face that I thought pretty much summed up my disgust.

"It's also a very important means of getting food," my dad went on. "If we're lucky, we'll catch enough today to grill up for dinner tonight."

"Mmm, delish!" said Jay.

I made another face. The only thing worse than catching fish was eating them, as far as I was concerned.

In the shack at the front of the pier, my dad bought some bait and paid our admission. Then we all walked down the wooden dock to claim our "spots." The pier was long, but already crowded. I couldn't believe so many people actually *paid* to do this. For fun! Early in the morning! Especially since fishing piers stink. A lot. There are fish guts and scales all over the place (plus a few cigars, and a lot of BO). Ugh!

Jay stared at me. "Egad! Are you okay?" he asked.

My hands were clapped over my nose and mouth. "I can't breathe!" I gagged.

"She'll get used to it," said my dad. (He's used to my reaction to fish smell, I guess.) He looked around, then grinned and set down his cooler and tackle box. "Here's a good place, don't you think?"

"Looks A-OK to me. Let the fishing commence!" Jay declared.

Let's get it over with already! I thought.

I took a pole and got ready to cast, then immediately jumped back. "Gross!" I cried. There was a dried fish head on the railing right in front of me!

"This is *not* a good place," I said, frowning. "I'm going over there, toward the end of the pier."

"Okay," said my dad, "but don't forget your bait."

Oh . . . right. How silly of me.

He held out two Styrofoam containers. "Squid or worms? What do you think?"

What did I think? What I thought was that I wanted to stay as far away as possible from both of those things.

"Gimme some worms!" said Josh, reaching in and grabbing a handful.

"Sweet! I'm taking squid!" said Brian. He picked one out of the cup and gave it a shake. Then he pretended to eat it. "Slurp, slurp. Yum!"

Really, really not funny.

"So which'll it be?" my dad asked me as Josh and Brian ran off down the pier.

"Uh . . ." I bit my lip and slowly reached my hand out toward one . . . and then the other. I so did not want either.

"Why don't you start with a worm?" suggested my dad.

I shrugged and took one. Then of course it had to go and *wiggle*. I jumped — and dropped it — and watched it fall through the slats of the pier.

"Or maybe a squid?" my dad said, raising an eyebrow.

"Here, allow me to pick the very best, and bait your hook for you," said Jay. He grinned and took a little bow. "It would be an honor."

"Thanks," I said, and I had to smile. Jay was totally weird. But he was also okay sometimes.

Once the baiting was done, the actual fishing part wasn't that bad. (Though no matter what my dad said, I did *not* get used to the smell.)

I actually liked casting. And just standing there dangling my line in the water gave me time to think about Jeremy Ryan and that one lifeguard, and which one was really cuter. (So hard to say!) And about Mina and Liza and what they were probably doing at that very moment. (Having a fabulous time, I was sure. Me, jealous? Yes.) I wondered if they'd gotten the packages I had sent a few days before, and when I'd be getting my souvenir packages from them. I thought about what flavor ice cream I was going to get when we were done fishing. (Cookie dough, maybe? Mint chocolate chip?) I thought about the pros and cons of Josh and Brian falling off the pier. (There were several of both.) And I thought about Juliette and wondered why she didn't seem to want to be my friend.

I also thought about how *slowly* time goes when you're fishing . . . almost as slowly as time at the Drift Inn. And I wondered if I'd catch anything at all that day.

Then, suddenly, I felt a tug on my pole that nearly jerked me out of my flip-flops.

"Hey!" I cried. "I think I caught something!"

I yanked back on the pole, grabbed for the handle, and tried my best to reel the line in. But the thing was not budging. In fact, it was pulling me forward! I took a step backward and tried again.

"Whoa, look!" said a guy to my left. "Looks like Junior's got a big one!"

Junior? Come on! I was wearing a halter top.

Unfortunately, I didn't have time to make sure that everyone knew I was, in fact, a girl. I was way too busy playing tug-of-war with my fishing line.

"Easy! Not too fast," said another man behind me. I glanced back. A whole crowd had suddenly formed.

"You got it," said another.

Yeah, but what did I have? A killer whale? Or maybe — and this would be typical — my hook was just caught on the dumb pier.

Just when I thought it couldn't be worth the battle, whatever it was, a flash of silver broke the surface. The whole pier erupted in cheers.

"That is one big fish, Samantha!" said my dad, appearing by my side. "Need any help?"

My hands and arms were killing me. "I can do it," I grunted.

My rod was bending almost to the breaking point, but I kept reeling and reeling the line in. Next thing I knew, a fish the size of Jay's Prius came flipping and flopping out of the water. (Okay, maybe it was a little smaller than that. But not much.)

"It's a monster!" cried one guy.

"It's a fighter, too!" someone else yelled.

Tell me about it, I thought. But now that the fish was out of the water, it seemed to have lost some of its fight. I stopped reeling and slowly walked backward, pulling the fish up and onto the pier.

There was a round of applause, and I almost took a bow.

"That's my girl!" said my dad.

As it turned out, not only had I caught the biggest fish so far that day, but I'd caught the biggest fish on the pier so far that summer! Someone ran out with a scale, which said that the thing weighed a whopping twenty-two pounds. They even took my picture with it, to hang in the bait shop.

"We're with her!" Josh and Brian actually bragged. (I figured it was the first and last time *that* would ever happen.)

Then my dad took a knife out to gut my fish.

"Hang on!" I cried.

"Do you want to do it?" he asked me.

"No!" I replied. Was he kidding?

"I didn't think so," he said. "But I have to do it here, or it'll go bad before we get home."

"What say we hang it in the Fish Room?" Jay suggested. "Next to the pompano!"

I shook my head.

Here's the thing: That fish very clearly wanted to keep living. I could tell. And when I looked at it, I couldn't help thinking about that fairy tale, the one about the fish who's really a wizard and can talk, and grants all those wishes to the fisherman, blah blah blah? Of course, it was clear that this fish couldn't talk. (He'd had his chance.) But still . . .

I stared hard into the fish's flat eyeball. *Please, please, please make this summer get better,* I silently begged.

Then I waved my hand. "Throw it back," I said to my dad.

I must admit, I kind of enjoyed the looks of disappointment on his and Jay's faces. "Don't worry," I assured them. "There are more fish in the sea, you know."

Jay grinned. "She speaketh the truth!"

And no, I didn't really believe the fish was magic . . . but sometimes a girl needs all the help she can get.

* * *

I didn't catch any more fish that day. But I did catch something else, by accident.

I was just casting my line again, when I felt it snag behind me. I heard a voice cry out, "Hey, careful! Watch it!"

I froze, then cringed and slowly turned around.

Oops. Just as I'd feared — my hook — worm and all — was stuck in some stranger's T-shirt.

I started to say, "I'm sorry," but froze again. It wasn't just some stranger. It was the cute lifeguard from the beach!

I thought I might die of humiliation. May I rest in peace.

"I — I am *so* sorry!" I blurted. "Really, *really* sorry!"

"Uh . . . it's okay," he said. He looked down at the slimy worm spot on his shirt and grinned. "If you want this shirt so badly, you can have it, I guess." Then he took the hook in his hand — just as Josh and Brian walked up, howling.

"Look!" Josh cried, pointing. "Sam caught another one!"

"Quick, get a picture!" Brian laughed. I guess they were back to their old selves.

The lifeguard turned to them. "Don't I know you guys?" he said.

Recognition flickered across Josh's and Brian's faces. They looked at each other quickly, then took off running across the pier.

The lifeguard looked at me, grinning. "I guess you know them, too," he said.

"Yeah . . ." I sighed. Unfortunately, I did. "That's my brother — my much *younger* brother," I added, "and his equally young friend."

"Oh yeah?" The lifeguard raised his sunglasses to his forehead, and I saw that his eyes were the exact same amazing blue as the shallow end of a swimming pool. "Oh, sure," he said. "I know you, too."

I couldn't help but break into a huge smile. I really hoped it didn't look too goofy. The lifeguard, meanwhile, pulled my hook out of his shirt and carefully handed it back to me. Then he grinned this grin that every boy in the world should practice.

"You guys swim at the beach where I work," he said. "Nice to meet you. I'm Nick."

"I know," I blurted.

"You do?"

"Oh, I mean, I didn't know your name was Nick.

Mine's Samantha. Nice to meet you! But I did know you were our lifeguard. Ten to eleven, one to two, and four to five. Right?" I said.

"Uh . . . just about, yeah," he answered.

I realized too late that he probably thought it was totally weird that I knew when his shifts were. I had to change the subject, and fast. "So, I'm really, *really* sorry I hooked you," I said.

"Oh, don't worry about it," he told me. "It's an old shirt — and just one of the hazards of fishing, I guess." He looked down at his dive watch. "I'd better get started myself." He reached for his own pole and nodded down the pier. "Wish me luck." He winked. Winked! "I'll see you soon, Samantha."

"See you soon, Nick!" I said.

As I watched him walk off, I couldn't help wondering if maybe I was dreaming all this. Did the cutest lifeguard in the world and I now really know each other by name?!

"Hey, sunshine, ready to go?" asked my dad, walking up with a fish-loaded cooler.

"Do we have to?" I sighed and looked longingly after Nick.

"Well, since we're all out of bait, I'm going to say yeah," my dad replied. "But I'm more than happy to bring you back tomorrow."

Thanks, but no thanks. "Okay. I'm coming. Just give me a sec."

As soon as he'd walked off, I turned to the railing, leaned over, and murmured, "Thank you, Mr. Fish!"

Chapter Seven

At last! My days of being bored out of my mind at the beach were over. It was like starting a whole new vacation — one where I was friends with the lifeguard!

The next morning, I could hardly wait to get out of the house, even though Nick wasn't on the stand yet. But I was ready when he got there . . . with Kiki and Emery by my side, as usual. (It actually wasn't *so* bad having them around. When Karen and Jay realized that I was entertaining them all the time, they started to pay me five dollars an hour! I was saving up for some more board shorts and a bikini — one that fit, this time.)

"Hi, Nick!" I said, appearing a few minutes after he sat down. (I had to play it cool, after all.)

"Oh, hi, Samantha. How're you doing? Are these your sisters?" he asked.

Kiki jumped up and down and nodded, and Emery started barking. Jeez.

"Oh no," I said.

Kiki crossed her arms and frowned.

"Actually, they're my mom's friend's kids," I explained. "This is Kiki." I patted her head and she waved. "And Emery." She wagged her invisible tail and panted.

"Nice to meet you guys," said Nick. Then he thoughtfully rubbed his chin. "So I guess you don't know the rules," he said, looking from one little girl to the other.

"What?" Kiki asked. She looked suddenly nervous. "Can't we pee in the ocean? My dad told me it's okay."

I cringed a little, but Nick just shook his head and grinned. Then he pointed to Emery. "No dogs on the beach," he said.

The girls' eyes grew wide — while I bit my lip to keep from laughing.

Kiki pulled Emery to her feet. "She's not *really* a dog!" she said.

Nick grinned at me, then at them. "Ah! Phew," he said. "I thought you guys were going to get me in trouble."

Kiki sighed — and I might have sighed, too. Nick the lifeguard was cute *and* had a good sense of humor. (Much better than Jeremy Ryan's, that was for sure.) *He might just be the perfect guy,* I thought.

A second later, though, a look of concern crossed Kiki's face again. "So is it okay to pee in the ocean?" she asked.

Nick nodded matter-of-factly. "It is," he said, "*if* you're at least five feet away from other swimmers."

"Got it!" said Kiki. "I'm gonna go tell Daddy!" And just like that, she and Emery raced off to the parents' semicircle of chairs, down the beach.

"I've got to thank you," I told Nick.

"Why?" he asked me.

"Because I'm in the water with them a lot," I said. "And we're usually way less than five feet apart."

He laughed and twirled his whistle. "Don't mention it."

"So did you catch anything at the pier yesterday?" I asked him. "I'm sorry I didn't say goodbye, but my dad suddenly got all, 'We've gotta go and get these fish on ice.'" I held up my hands and shook them, like my dad does when he gets antsy.

Nick chuckled. "Oh, that's okay. I caught a few small ones," he said. "But did I see your picture up on the bulletin board when I left?"

I'm sure my giant smile at that moment set some sort of personal record.

"Yes, you did!" I said, turning beet red despite my thick layer of SPF 40.

"Hey, Chip!" He turned to another guard who was walking up with a big orange umbrella. He looked a little older, and not quite as cute, but he had an excellent tan. "Guess what?" Nick told him. "This girl just caught the biggest fish yet this season down at the pier. A twenty-two-pound mackerel!"

"No kidding!" Chip said. He passed the umbrella up to Nick, then high-fived me with both hands. "Dude! You rock!"

Dude! I thought. *This summer suddenly rocks, too!*

If only Liza and Mina had been there with me, it would have been truly perfect. I know they're a little shier than I am, but they would have loved Nick and the other lifeguards. Not only was there Chip, who was starting college that fall, but there was also Lexy, who could do backflips (and who was Chip's girlfriend, too). Plus Caleb, and Tate, and Jasmine . . . who used to live in New

Jersey, also! It was so funny — all this time I'd been looking around for *someone* to hang out with. And they were right in front of me the whole time, on the lifeguard stand!

I honestly wasn't sure which was better: making new friends, or finally having a foolproof way to get Josh and Brian to leave me alone. (Even they knew better than to pull their annoying pranks right in front of a lifeguard.) Now when Juliette finally came out to the beach in the afternoons, I almost didn't notice. I was just so happy to be treated like a teenager by Nick and his friends, even if Juliette still wouldn't give me the time of day.

(And, okay, I might have let them think that I was thirteen, not twelve. But turning twelve honestly seemed so long ago already. . . .)

Anyway, the summer was really, truly looking up! And to make it even better, I got a big envelope from Mina a few days later — which included not only a three-page (!) letter, but also a gift: sheet music for my guitar with all kinds of cute paintings by Mina in the margins. (She is so talented. Really!) I guess Mina assumed I might have learned how to play the thing already. (And who would blame her?) Unfortunately, I had not. Still, I immediately grabbed the music — it was "Under the Boardwalk," an old 60s song — got out my guitar, and headed to the back porch to give it a shot.

"Hey, cool ax!" said Jay, walking out the back door a few minutes later.

"Excuse me?" I said.

He nodded toward my instrument. "El guitar, mi amiga." He grinned. "I didn't know you were a musician. Brava!" he said.

I shrugged. "Well . . . I'm not, really. Not yet, anyway."

"Let's hear what you've got so far," he said, sitting down at the picnic table.

So I put my fingers where the little black dots on the chord diagram told me to and strummed. I wasn't exactly sure how it should have sounded . . . but I was pretty sure it should have sounded better than it did.

I sighed. "It's not the best guitar in the world, I guess."

Jay nodded and reached out a hand. "May I?" he asked.

"Uh, sure," I said. I handed my "ax" over to him.

The first thing Jay did was hold up the guitar and look it over. Then he put his foot on the porch railing and set the guitar on his knee. He leaned his ear toward the neck and, making a dozen different, totally weird faces, began plucking each string and turning the tuning keys carefully.

"Just a wee bit out of tune. There," he said, strumming all six strings smoothly a few times. Then he broke into a crazy-amazing solo I couldn't even follow, his hands moved so fast. After a minute, he strummed one final chord, took a goofy bow, and handed it back to me. "Try it now," he said.

"How did you do that?" I asked. My mouth was definitely hanging open. "You play really, really well!"

"Ah, that's nothing," he said modestly. "Bass was really my thing, back in the day when I had my band."

Jay may have been cooler than I'd given him credit for. "What kind of band?" I asked him. *Marching? Or wandering minstrel?* That was just about all I could picture.

"Just your average rock and roll band," he explained, grinning. "We called ourselves Noise Party. But that was before I found my true calling . . . renaissance fairs."

Right. Rock band vs. renaissance fairs. Clearly a no-brainer.

Jay looked down at the sheet music on the table in front of me. "What are you playing there, anyway?" he asked.

"Oh, it's called 'Under the Boardwalk,'" I said. "My friend Mina sent it to me. She's the one who added all the drawings. We always used to play under the boardwalk at the beach when we were little, so it's kind of funny." I pointed to one picture. "I think that's supposed to be us. Too bad there's no boardwalk at *this* beach. . . ." I shrugged. "It's too hard a song for me to play, anyway."

"Au contraire!" Jay said quickly. He pointed to the sheet music. "It's an easy chord change, really. 'Under the boardwalk' — E major — 'out of the sun, under the boardwalk' — D — 'we'll be having some fun.' Would you like me to show you?"

By dinnertime, I'd learned the whole song — and had taught Kiki most of the words! I practically had my own little band. So what if my lead singer was five years old?

Then that night, we played miniature golf again — at the course with the giant volcano this time, finally — and I got a hole in one at the end, so I won a free game! (Despite Josh's and Brian's very best attempts at sabotage.)

Talk about luck changing! My summer was

clearly looking up. *I should have gone fishing weeks ago,* I thought.

As for Nick, as the days went on, I found out a ton of things about him. His full name was Nicholas Coleman Davis and he was sixteen years old. He lived in Wilmington, North Carolina, but he spent every summer at his family's beach cottage, which had the funny name: Conch-ed Out. This was his first year working as a lifeguard and he liked it a lot. Baseball and basketball were his favorite sports. He did *not* have a girlfriend. (And even though he was tan, he could still blush.) Oh, and he got his cool rope bracelet at the other surf shop on the island. (I was *so* going there with my mom!)

And there was one more thing: According to Nick, all of the lifeguards thought the Drift Inn was haunted.

"Really?" I asked him one afternoon on the beach when he told me. I could almost believe it — though I didn't want to!

He shrugged. "I don't know. That's just what they say."

I couldn't help it. My mouth fell open. *Haunted? Oh no!* (Not that anyone really believes in that stuff, of course.)

Then Nick laughed. "No, no. I'm just kidding."

Oh.

I laughed, too, and tried my best to play it off. "Of course you were."

Phew!

I considered going back to the fishing pier on Nick's next day off. And this was *after* my dad had gone back to New Jersey! But when I asked Nick if he was going, he told me he didn't think so.

"I'm going to go surfing," he said, "now that the wind is offshore and the waves have kicked up by the inlet."

"You can *surf* around here?" I asked. I looked out at the ocean and the one-foot-tall "whitecaps" rolling in.

"Well, not here," Nick said, looking out at the calm water. "But down the beach about a mile. I mean, it's no Maui or Australia or anything, but it's better than nothing. Ever surf before?" he asked. "Maybe you should check it out!"

Chapter Eight

I explained the whole surfing beach thing to my mom the next morning, and it only took a little begging to get her to agree to let me go. (She even took me to the surf shop to get a rash guard and a rope bracelet, just like Nick's!) As soon as we got back, I headed down the beach and quickly realized that it was a walk I should have taken long before. Sure, there was no boardwalk, just old houses and beach grass, sea oats and dunes. But each section of beach had its own unique *appeal*, you could say.

There was our beach, designed exclusively for the zero-to-six-year-old set. But there were also stretches of beach filled with newlyweds and other adults who were still young enough to run around, plus one that seemed to be full of people with gray hair (or *no* hair) on their heads. There was one place that was all surf fishermen, standing knee-deep in the waves with their lines out, and one stretch that was just for dogs and their Frisbee-throwing people. There was even one beach that, to my surprise, was completely empty except for a sign that said, NO PLAYING OR BATHING — LOGGERHEAD TURTLE NESTING AREA.

The sun was blistering, as usual, but bearable if I kept my feet where the waves could reach them. Then again, to get where I was going, I would probably have walked across the sun. I felt free, and grown-up, and like I was on a true vacation — for the first time in a month.

At last, I rounded a corner and could see several figures bobbing and paddling in the water. I felt my heart actually leap up. It was like I had discovered my own New World! (I would not be surprised at all to learn that Columbus felt the exact same way back in 1492.)

It took a while to find Nick, because surfers all look pretty much the same when they're out in the water. In fact, the first person I recognized was another lifeguard, Jasmine — because there were fewer girls in the water, and because no one else in the world could have hair as curly and long as hers was.

Then another wave rolled in. A few surfers chased it, and one with wet brown hair popped up on his board. As soon as he was up, I could see that it was Nick, and I got this weird feeling of pride as I watched him ride the wave in.

When the wave broke, he jumped off his board and landed waist-deep in the water.

"Hey, Nick!" I called, raising both arms and waving them wildly. "Over here!"

He shielded his eyes with his hand and gazed around until he saw me. Then he waved back, and my heart jumped once more. He walked out of the surf, grinning and shaking his hair out, with his board under one arm. He was wearing a blue-and-green rash guard and bright yellow shorts.

"Hey," he called. "You came. What, no board?"

I smiled. "I told you, I've never surfed before."

"So do you want to learn?" he asked.

Do I ever! "Well . . ." I pretended to think about it. "Why not? Sure!" I promptly jogged off toward the water. What were we waiting for?

"Hey, hang on!" I heard Nick call. I turned around just in time to see him gently lay down his board. "Before you dive right in," he said, "let's practice a few things on the sand first."

I shrugged. "If you say so."

It wasn't like I'd never been on a boogie board or anything, but whatever. A little practice never hurt anyone. And I tried — I really did! — to pay attention as Nick demonstrated how to lie on the board and paddle, one arm at a time, and then stand up.

"Okay," he said when he'd finished. "Now it's your turn."

I lay down on the board and put my arms right by my rib cage.

"Perfect," he told me.

I grinned and flutter-kicked a little. *Thank you very much!*

"Okay, keep your chin up and pretend you feel the wave under you," he went on. "Now push your chest up and slide your feet under you. . . ."

"Like this?" I said, jumping to my feet.

"Almost," Nick said. "But try to land your foot right where your belly button was. And make sure you stay on the stringer —"

"The *what?*" I asked.

"This line right here, down the middle of the board." He pointed to it.

"Right. Got it," I said, and tried it again. I nailed it! "Ta-da!"

Nick laughed. "Pretty good. But, hey, do you mean to be goofy?"

Goofy? My arms fell to my sides. "Oh, sorry," I said. I do try to be goofy, sometimes. But I definitely wasn't going for that just then.

Nick pointed to my feet and, grinning his super-white smile, slowly shook his head. "What I mean is, do you naturally stand like that, with your right foot out in front?" he said.

I sighed (with relief!). "Oh yeah," I said. "Like in snowboarding." I suddenly remembered the term *goofy* coming up on a ski trip the year before. (I am definitely learning to snowboard next year, by the way. I learned to ski because that's what my parents do. But snowboarding gear is so much cuter!) "I guess I am goofy," I told Nick. "I'm left-footed in soccer, even though I write with my right hand. My coach says it makes me a great forward. But is it okay to surf that way, too, do you think?"

Nick nodded. "Yeah, no problem."

Phew!

"So?" I asked eagerly. "Can I go out and really surf now?"

He looked me over once more and pressed down gently on my shoulders. "Okay," he said, "but remember to keep your knees bent and your body low. Stand straight up, and you'll wipe out," he warned.

"Got it." I nodded and crouched down *very* low. Then I held my arms out to the sides and pretended to ride a huge wave.

Those itty-bitty waves I was looking at had better watch out!

There were a few things I took away from the surfing beach when I left two hours later. (I'd promised Kiki I'd go back and build a sand castle — with a pool *and* a Zen rock garden — for her Polly Pockets after lunch.)

One: Even little, itty-bitty waves can pack a serious punch. As Nick and his fellow surfers would say, not only did I wipe out; I got "worked"!

Two: It hurts to "pearl" and go "over the falls" (which basically means that your feet are too far forward on your board, and there's no way you can stay up). I should know. I did it a lot.

Three: Nick was an excellent teacher, because after five, or six, or maybe seven tries, I was *almost* standing up. (A possible record, he told me!)

And four: I was stoked to snowboard in the winter, because Nick said it's exactly like surfing — and surfing is *fun*!

Thanks to Nick, even on my own stretch of beach, I finally had something to do besides sit in pits of sand surrounded by preschoolers. (But no, that didn't stop completely. It was hard to say "no" to Kiki — and five dollars an hour. I don't know if I had finally gotten used to it, but somehow it didn't seem like such a chore anymore.)

On top of my new hobby, Nick actually let me do some real lifeguard work when he was on duty. I mean, it was just piling sand in front of the stand and propping the foam rescue cans up, but it was still fun. Which was why I noticed right away when, one morning at ten, he didn't show.

"Hey, Chip. Hey, Lexy," I said. They were both sitting on the stand, looking out over the water. "Where's Nick?" I asked them.

Lexy smiled at me and pointed way out in the distance, where I could just barely see a head bobbing in the water. I knew the lifeguards liked to swim out far, but I'd never seen them way out there. Was that really Nick? And was that even allowed?

I waved, and for a second I thought I saw him waving back. But then his hand kept on waving, and the other one started up, too. That was weird.

Maybe he was just happy to see me? Or — it hit me suddenly in the gut, like a jab from Josh — was he waving for *help*?

No, I thought to myself. He was way too good of a swimmer. But his hands kept waving . . . and the next second, Chip jumped up.

Nick was in trouble!

The next thing I knew, Chip was blowing his whistle like crazy, and immediately, a whole series of whistles sounded along the beach. Lexy, meanwhile, had a rescue tube over her shoulder and had leapt off the stand onto the sand pile, and was now charging toward the waves as fast as she possibly could. A second later, Tate and Caleb appeared out of nowhere with rescue tubes of their own, and followed her.

I stood there, frozen, dying to do something — anything! — to help. But all I could do was watch as Lexy, and then Tate, swam out to Nick.

Hurry! I silently pleaded. *Hurry, hurry, hurry! You've got to save him!*

It seemed to take forever, but at last Lexy reached him. It looked like she wrapped the tube around Nick's chest, by which time Tate had joined them. Caleb, meanwhile, stood on the shore holding a rope that ran all the way to Tate and

Lexy. They gave him a signal, and very quickly, hand over hand, he began to pull.

By then, there were a dozen lifeguards waiting at the water's edge, plus a stretcher (oh no!), and a crowd of kids and parents wondering what was going on. The lifeguard whistles were still blowing, blowing, blowing . . . making the whole scene seem even worse!

At last, Lexy and Tate reached the shore with Nick between them. They rose to their feet and dragged his limp body out of the water to the dry sand and laid him down.

Get up! Get up, Nick! I thought. But he didn't move.

No! It wasn't possible! Sure, I'd gotten lectures about riptides, and I'd even seen the guards help a few swimmers out of them. But I'd never really thought that the ocean could be so dangerous. And I'd *never* imagined someone I knew — especially a lifeguard! — could get into trouble out there.

Suddenly, I couldn't feel the scalding sand, or the sun beating down on me anymore. As for everything inside me, it felt like some intestinal supernova had turned it all into a black hole. I was just a shell as I watched Nick lie there, with the lifeguards all around him. For the first time in weeks, I didn't feel hot. I just felt small and scared and cold.

I covered my eyes. I couldn't watch them do CPR — or whatever!

And that was when the claps and the cheers broke out.

I opened my eyes slowly . . . just in time to see Nick jumping up with a giant smile on his face. *What?!* Then — this was even harder to process — he and Lexy and Tate and Caleb all took a big bow.

"Woo-hoo!" several people cheered.

"Great drill, everybody," said an older man wearing an orange hat and holding a stopwatch. "Four minutes. Good time, Lexy. Next time, Nick, it's your turn."

I was trying to understand what had just happened (and trying to breathe again, I admit) as Nick walked by and waved cheerfully.

"Are . . . are you okay?" I asked slowly. I regretted it right away.

Nick kind of laughed. "Did you really think I was in trouble?" he said.

"What? Me?" I made an "as if" face and blurted, "Of course not!"

I was glad that my insides seemed to have jelled. The world around me was coming back into focus. But I was not enjoying the feeling of that hot, hot sun again.

Nick reached out and patted my shoulder. "Good. You looked a little freaked-out. Hey, the water's great, you know. You should go in."

Chapter Nine

Thankfully, it didn't take me long to get over the whole Nick-rescue drama. In fact, by that afternoon, I was totally feeling like myself again, and was rather proud of designing a pretty cool mini-golf course on the beach for Kiki and her little friends. Plus, I'd had a pretty impressive rescue of my own before lunch. Not quite as dramatic as Lexy's . . . but *real* at least, thank you very much!

It all started when Josh and Brian raced by me with a pack of preschoolers on their heels.

"Give me back my bucket!" Kiki hollered on the verge of tears. "I'm telling Mom! Give it!"

Brian stopped for a second and dangled a pink plastic pail in front of him. "Why don't you come and get it?" he taunted.

Kiki ran up and lunged, but Brian yanked it away. "Too slow!" he teased her.

"Suckers!" yelled Josh. "Hey, Bri, what do you say we chuck it all in the ocean?"

"No!" cried the kids.

Brian nodded, grinning wickedly. "I'm in!"

I sighed. Enough was enough. Without a word, I stomped over to Josh's towel and found just what I was looking for. Then I jogged back to the surf.

"Out of our way!" Josh yelled, coming up behind me.

I held up his DS case. "I think maybe you should stop," I warned him. "More than one can play that game, you know." I slowly began to swing the case to and fro.

Josh's mouth dropped open. "You wouldn't!"

I looked at him and grinned. I really thought he knew me better than that.

"Just give back the toys," I said, nodding to the line of victims, "and pick on someone your own size from now on."

The boys hesitated, so I stepped out to where the water rolled over my toes. "Now!" I commanded.

Josh turned to Brian nervously. "Do what she says," he gulped.

And together, they dropped their booty.

Kiki and her friends dove in to claim it. "Yay for Samantha!" Kiki cheered.

Grinning, I tossed Josh's case up to the dry sand and brushed off my hands.

He frowned as he scooped it up. "You are messed up, Sam," he said.

"I know you are, Josh, but what am I?" I said, just as Kiki wrapped her arms around my waist in a giant hug.

Still, despite my accomplishments for the day, when I went to bed that night, I couldn't get to sleep.

Maybe it was just because my room was so hot — a thick, heavy heat that made my bed feel like rocks in a sauna. Or maybe it was because my mind was buzzing with thoughts, and I just couldn't stop them.

Some — okay, a lot — were about Nick and what had happened that morning. No matter how hard I tried, I kept seeing the same thing over and over: him lying as limp as those moon jellies Josh loves to collect. Then my thoughts started to shift a little. They were still on Nick . . . but now they were about how much I liked him. I hadn't really admitted it before, but I definitely had a crush on him. Could he be crushing on me, too?

He was awfully nice to me. But he was sixteen and I was still just twelve. My parents would never, ever let me go out with him (or anyone else, for that matter!). So what if he did like me back? What would happen then? And what would I tell Jeremy Ryan when I got home again?

If only I'd had Mina and Liza to talk to! Oh, well . . .

On top of all that, there was a part of me that couldn't help — late at night, in creepy room 13 — thinking about what Nick had said about the house being haunted. Sure, he was joking. But my mom always says that every joke has a little truth behind it. And all of a sudden, the big, old place suddenly seemed like an awfully good home for ghosts — what with the full moon leering in at me, and the waves sounding just like a growling monster right outside. (Bottom line: I should not have read *Appointment with Death* before bed. Big mistake!)

I turned my pillow over for the hundredth time to find a cool spot, tightly shut my eyes, and ordered myself to go to sleep.

And that was when I heard it.

It wasn't the waves, and I didn't think it was the wind either. It sounded like a ghostly soul, crying in utter torment!

My eyes flew open and it stopped. I took a deep breath.

Then it started again.

If I'd had any covers on top of me, I definitely would have pulled them up over my head. I curled up in a ball instead. I was just thankful that whatever was making that sound seemed to be staying where it was.

Then it hit me like a rogue wave! That sound was coming through the wall just behind me. And that meant one thing: It was coming from Juliette's room.

Should I run over there and try, somehow, to save her?

Or should I silently wish her luck and dive under my bed?

Or were the sounds I was hearing not zombie moans at all, but maybe . . . sobs?

Duh! I thought. Juliette was crying! And the minute I realized that, I jumped up and ran to her door.

But then I stopped short. No matter how much I wanted to knock and ask Juliette what was wrong, I couldn't help thinking: *Why would she talk to me now, when she never really has before?*

I stood there for what seemed like ages, trying to figure out what to do.

What if I'd been crying for so long? I finally wondered. *Would I really want to be left alone? Or would I want someone to rub my back and tell me I'm not alone?* I knew the answer — for me, at least. And so what if Juliette said, "Get lost!"? *Again.* At least I would have showed I cared. At least I would have done *something*.

So I raised my fist and knocked very gently on the door. Then I held my breath and braced for a very possible "Leave me alone!"

There was a pause, then a very faint, *Sniff, sniff.* "Who is it?"

I turned the knob and pushed the door slowly. There was a soft creak as it opened.

"Uh, hi . . . it's Samantha," I whispered.

The moon was bright in Juliette's room, too, and I could see her lying on her bed in a ball just like I had been. Her ceiling fan was whirring softly, and everything was fluttering: the loose wallpaper, the cockeyed shades, the sheets, even her hair. She had her back to me, and I was surprised at how small she looked. Suddenly, I felt like I'd made a mistake. Maybe I didn't belong there after all.

But then Juliette spoke again in a voice that was high and tight and about as miserable as one can get. "What do you want?" she asked.

"I . . . uh . . . well . . . nothing really. I mean, I guess I just wanted to see if you were okay. I, um, heard you through the wall. And if you want to talk or anything . . . I just wanted you to know I'm up. But I completely understand if you want to be alone, and I'm really sorry for bothering you." I swallowed hard. "Really. I'll just go now. Good night." I tiptoed backward.

Slowly, Juliette turned around. "No, wait . . . That's okay," she said hoarsely.

I could see right away that her face was all puffed up and blotchy. She'd been crying, all right. But why? I crossed the floor and touched her gently on the shoulder.

"Do you . . . want to talk about it?" I asked her.

"There's nothing to say," she choked. "I hate them both!"

"Who?" I asked as a million ideas raced through my mind all at once. The first thought, of course, was Josh and Brian. But I hadn't really noticed them bothering her that much. (That privilege seemed to be exclusively mine. Lucky me.) Or maybe she meant a boyfriend? I thought she'd said she didn't have one. But maybe I was wrong. (Once in a while, that happened.) Maybe she had a terrible boyfriend. Or maybe she had an Olivia Miner stealing him out from under her.

She sucked in a trembly breath. "My parents," she muttered.

Oh. I nodded. Of course. "What did they do?"

Juliette looked up at me, surprised. "Don't you know?" she said. She scooted over a little. "Uh, here, sit down."

"No, I don't know," I said as I took a seat, and more thoughts raced through my head. Were they sending her to another school? Or had they grounded her for life? But Jackie didn't seem that mean. And Juliette's dad wasn't even around.

"They're doing it," she went on, clearly trying to hold back a sob. "It's really happening. They're splitting up. After twenty years. Can you believe it? How can they do that? I hate them so much!"

Wait. What? Splitting up?

I couldn't believe it. And I didn't know what to say at all. "Did you . . ." I began, ". . . uh, just find out?"

Juliette sniffed. "Not really. I mean, I knew they were having problems. That's why my dad didn't come to the beach with us. But they said they were going to try to work things out. My dad even said he'd try to come for a week in August. Then today he calls and says he got his own apartment! Not only is he not coming; he's not even going to be there when we get home!" With that, her sobs began to pour out all over again.

"I . . . I'm so sorry, Juliette," I said, wishing so badly that I could think of something to say that would make her feel a little better. I tried to think about how I'd feel if that happened to my parents, but I couldn't. My parents were my parents — they went together, like the yin-yang symbols on the necklace I sent Liza. Still, I knew it could happen, and *had* happened to people like Zoe Martin. But she actually seemed okay with it now, after a year.

"It'll be okay," I said, rubbing Juliette's arm gently. "I know it doesn't seem like it. But really, it will."

Juliette didn't say anything else, and I didn't either. But I thought about all the things I could say . . . like how great it could be now to have double holidays, vacations, and maybe even wardrobes. Like how sometimes single parents (like Zoe's dad) let you get away with a whole lot more.

But it's weird — sometimes the less you say, the better. And for once, I didn't go on and on. I just hugged Juliette and let her cry some more.

*   *   *

We didn't get much sleep that night.

Juliette didn't say much at first, but after a while she did start telling me how hard the summer had been, worrying about her parents, missing her dad, and being away from all her friends for so long.

"My mom says she needs this time," Juliette explained. "But" — she looked around — "it's the last thing that I need. Being away from my friends, and surrounded by other . . . happy families. It feels like this summer will never end! I should have stayed with my dad," she said.

"Why didn't you?" I asked her.

She wiped her eyes. "He said he was just too busy with work and . . . looking for a new place to live, I guess."

A new wave of tears appeared. "I'm sorry," she sobbed. "My summer's ruined, but I don't want to ruin yours, too."

"Don't be sorry!" I told her. "I understand. And believe me, you are not ruining my summer. Not at all."

I hated to say it, but I was just a little, very teeny, tiny bit happy. Happy that Juliette hadn't been blowing me off. She'd just had a lot on her mind, that was all. And now she was

talking to me. In her room. About the most important things ever.

"I know it's really hard," I said. "But if it helps
you to talk, I'm totally here."

"Thanks, Samantha," Juliette said. She used
her pillow to wipe her eyes. "You're really cool.
I'm glad our moms are friends."

"Me too," I said. And I was. Very.

"You're lucky," she went on.

"Oh, my parents aren't perfect," I said quickly.

"No, it's not that," she said. "You get along so
easily with everyone. You've really — I don't
know — come out of your shell since the last time
I saw you. I envy that."

"You do?" I said. I couldn't have been more
surprised if she'd revealed that she was an alien
from the planet Xorba.

"Yeah, I do," she replied. "I wish I were more
fun, like you."

"But you are fun!"

She looked at me. "You're kidding, right?"

I shrugged. "Well, maybe not so much this summer. But I remember our moms' reunion. You
were the *most* fun then. Remember? Ou-yay aught-
tay e-may ig-pay atin-lay?"

Juliette nodded. "Es-yay. I loved doing your

115

hair there, too. It was so long." She studied my new look. "It looks supercute short. What made you decide to cut it?"

"Locks of Love," I explained.

"What's that?" she asked. I filled her in.

"That's awesome," she said. "See, Samantha? You *are* cool." Juliette pulled her own hair in front of her face. "Do you think mine's long enough?"

"We can measure it to check," I said. "It's got to be a foot. But I think so."

She let her hair go and flipped it back. "Awesome. I want to do it."

"Are you sure?" I asked. I mean, getting rid of my hair had been no big deal. But Juliette's was so pretty. So *her*.

"Definitely," Juliette replied. "I'm ready for a change."

"Well, it's definitely cooler when you have it short," I told her. I tilted my head up toward the ceiling. "And so is your room." I sighed. "You're lucky that your fan works." I shut my eyes and let the warm but steady breeze blow across my face.

"Yours doesn't?" she said. "Why didn't you change rooms?"

Good question. There were still plenty of empty bedrooms. But I'd already unpacked and put up pictures and settled in before I realized my mistake. And I still liked having Juliette next door.

But I didn't say that.

"I like the wallpaper," I said.

"Well, if you get too hot," said Juliette, "you can always come to my room."

"How about if I get scared?" I asked, glad at the chance to bring up a new subject. "You know what I've heard? This house might be haunted! Guess who told me?"

"Who?" asked Juliette.

"The lifeguard, Nick!" I said.

"Who?" She looked back at me blankly.

"The lifeguard," I told her. "Remember? The one I pointed out at the beach a while ago. Cute, with light brown hair. The one who got rescued in that drill today." Not that I wanted to think about *that* anymore. Then I remembered it had been early. "Oh, right. You weren't up. Never mind — it was just a drill. The one I talk to so much," I said.

"Oh, right." Juliette nodded. "You do talk to him a lot. And he is cute." She *almost* smiled. "See," she went on. "That's what I'm talking about. You make making friends look so easy."

"Well," I replied, grinning, "I think meeting Nick had more to do with catching him on my hook than with being outgoing. . . ." When she looked at me strangely, I told her the fishing pier story.

She was laughing before it was over, so I started telling her about my surfing lessons, too.

"You should totally come with me next time!" I said. "Nick could teach you, also. And there are a lot of other cool kids there, too. Don't blame yourself for not meeting anyone at *this* beach." I rolled my eyes toward the window. "It's like elementary school central, right?"

Juliette nodded. "Yeah, I've noticed. And yeah . . . I'd love to try surfing." A smile lingered on her face, and I noticed that her eyes were almost dry. Then her eyebrows slid together. "That lifeguard doesn't think this house is *really* haunted, does he?" she asked.

I shook my head quickly. "No . . . but when I first heard you crying, I almost thought he was right," I said.

"Sorry." Juliette squeezed my hand. "I'll try not to scare you anymore. But yes, you can come in here if you're scared. Or *any*time, really. I wish I'd talked to you sooner, Samantha," she said.

I didn't even know how to respond. All I knew was that I suddenly felt warmer — in a good way, for once!

*   *   *

By the time the sun was all the way up, I was wide awake. Juliette was sound asleep, so I slipped off the bed and quietly tiptoed out of the room. I had some business to attend to.

"Mom!" I said, walking out onto the porch. I pulled her up off of her yoga mat and dragged her into the Fish Room.

"What is it?" she asked me. "Is something wrong? What did Josh do?"

"Why didn't you tell me about Juliette's mom and dad?" I said, facing her and crossing my arms. "Did you think it wouldn't come up over the course of, what, two months?"

She sighed. "Well, honestly, Samantha, you haven't been around to talk to very much. You're either playing with the girls, or with the other kids you've met, or you have your nose buried in a book. There's only so much I can tell you if you don't have time to listen. Plus, I didn't know myself until we got here. But you're right, and I'm sorry. I should have found a time to explain everything to you."

I opened my mouth, then closed it. It's so confusing when your parents actually agree with you.

"So did Juliette tell you?" my mom asked.

I nodded.

"Good," she said. "I'm glad she's opening up a little. Jackie's been so worried about her. She's taking this so hard."

"Well, wouldn't you?" I asked.

She smiled a little. "Yes, I guess I would. But don't worry," she said quickly. "Nothing's going to happen to Daddy and me."

"Oh, I know *that*," I said. I hadn't even been thinking about that . . . until right then! (Thanks a lot, Mom.)

"But parents do split up sometimes," my mom went on, "and it's usually for the best in the long run, I suppose."

I made some kind of face that pretty much said, *Oh yeah? Really?*

"It's true," my mom said. "And I'm glad you finally know, because I really think you can help Juliette by being her friend. Maybe you can introduce her to some of your new friends, too. Some of those lifeguards seem just about her age. She could even go surfing with you next time."

She flashed one of those smiles of hers that basically said, "I am a genius." But I held up my hand.

"Way ahead of you, Mom," I said.

She reached out and hugged me. "I should have

known. I'm so proud of you, Samantha," she said. "Now, how about a little yoga?"

I hugged her back and looked over her shoulder, through the door, and out to sea. It would be another sweltering, sizzling, blistering day, I could already tell. But in so many other ways, it was going to be different.

"How about we ask Karen if we can wait for Juliette?" I suggested.

Chapter Ten

I probably shouldn't take *all* the credit for finally getting Juliette's vacation started . . . but I will! By the time my dad got back to the beach the next week, Juliette had not only met all my new friends and learned to surf, but cut off her hair and mailed it to Locks of Love, too. (She even let me do the honors, and it turned out pretty awesome.)

The funny thing was, my dad had just as much to say about the changes in *me* as about the changes in Juliette.

"Look how light your hair's gotten, and how much it's grown. And you're so tan — especially in that dress!" he said. (I was wearing an awesome rainbow-colored sundress that Juliette had loaned me.) "Are you using enough sunscreen? Every time I see you, sunshine, you look different, I swear!" he declared.

If you say so, Dad.

I guessed I'd upped my "surfer girl" wardrobe a little, thanks to the five dollars an hour from Karen, and Sonny's Surf Shop, *and* Juliette's generous closet. It turned out that she and I were the same size in some things, and she was absolutely, positively great about sharing clothes. We even traded bikinis: She looked amazing in the skull one that had traumatized me, and she gave me an excellent aqua one that was too small for her. (And yes, it stayed up!) As for all my Goth stuff, I packed most of it away, and gave the tutus to Kiki for dress-up.

Juliette also painted my nails the same bright blue as hers. That didn't go unnoticed by Kiki, of course, who immediately demanded we paint hers, also. Which then meant doing Emery's. (We had to call it "paw polish" for her, though.)

It actually started to feel like we were all sisters, like the March girls in *Little Women*, and I, of course, was Jo! (Only we lived in a big, questionably haunted beach house . . . and the youngest one of us preferred to bark instead of talk.)

But still, it was perfect.

Almost.

My dad, unfortunately, didn't get to stay for long. The reason? The weather. As usual.

"Just got a call from the station," he told us the day after he'd arrived. "They need me down in Florida to cover Hurricane Brian if it hits, which" — he got a gleam in his eye — "it looks like it will!"

"Hurricane *Brian*?" said Karen. She looked down at the puddles of ketchup and mayonnaise and who knows what else that her son had left on the porch after lunch. "How did they know?" she exclaimed. Everyone laughed.

"Oh, but Marv," my mom said and sighed. "You can't go. It's your vacation."

"Yeah, Dad, you just got here," I said (or rather, whined).

My dad shook his head cheerfully. "Mother Nature doesn't —"

"Take vacations," my mom and I flatly finished for him. (We'd last heard this saying over spring vacation, when my dad had had to leave early to cover the Midwestern floods.)

"Well put," said my dad, grinning. "I'll be back before you know it. Besides, I'm not going any-where yet. Not until late tomorrow. And I noticed on the way in from the airport that there's a carnival on the mainland. You guys haven't gone yet, have you? I think we should go tonight."

I love, love, love, love carnivals! And not just because of the rides — though I do love those. But also because of the food. I could live on funnel cakes and cotton candy if I had to, no problem at all.

And caramel apples with rainbow sprinkles. How could I forget those?

I'd been to enough carnivals, though, to know that you can't eat everything you want at once (and still enjoy riding the Spider), so I paced myself and had one funnel cake. Then it was ride time.

Josh and Brian were already off with Jay and my dad, thank goodness. The minute they'd seen that there were go-karts, they were all over that. My mom and Karen and Jackie, meanwhile, headed to the kiddy rides with Emery. But Kiki said that was way too babyish, and I really couldn't argue with her. So that left her with me and Juliette.

The only problem was, besides the Giant Slide and House of Fun, Kiki was too short to go on most of the rides with us. (No matter how hard she begged the operators . . . and she did.)

"Well," I said as we stood outside the Spider. "I

guess we'll have to take turns. You go first, Juliette, and I'll wait here with Kiki."

Juliette looked up at the arms spinning wildly overhead. "You know what?" she said. "I think I'll skip it, Samantha. You go ahead."

"Okay," I sighed, and walked up and handed the guy my ticket. But my heart wasn't in it. I love going on rides — but I don't love going on them alone. (There's no one to scream with! And you slide around too much.)

But then, just as I'd resigned myself to sitting alone — or even worse, with some sweaty stranger! — I spotted Nick in the crowd.

"Nick!" I cried. "Hey, Nick! Come ride this with me!" He saw me, waved, shrugged, and pulled out a ticket to join me.

If I said that was the best ride of my life, I would totally be lying. (The new roller coaster at Great Adventure was extremely hard to beat.) But it was still pretty great.

"I'm so glad I found you!" I told Nick as we climbed off the Spider a few minutes later. "I hate riding these things alone. Don't you? Wasn't that awesome? Want to ride it again?"

He grinned, but shook his head as he gently rubbed his ear. "I think I should find my friends," he said, "and let my hearing recover a little."

Oops.

"Sorry," I said sheepishly. "I guess I can scream a little loud."

He nodded. "A little," he said. "But I don't think there's any permanent damage."

I had to smile. "Maybe later?" I said (hopefully).

He nodded. "Sure," he said. Then he looked around us. "So, did you come here by yourself? Didn't, uh, anybody come with you?"

"Oh yeah," I said quickly. "The whole gang is here. But we've all split up — *fortunately* — and right now it's Juliette, me, and Kiki. She's not really big enough to go on much," I said as I led him off the platform and into the crowd. "There they are. Hey, guys," I called. "Check it out! Look who I found!"

"Hi," said Juliette, looking surprised.

Kiki looked surprised, too — but for a different reason. "Are you the lifeguard? You're wearing clothes. You look different," she told Nick.

He laughed. Then I waved good-bye. "Maybe we'll see you later," I said (hopefully again). "I know you have to find your friends."

"Huh?" He glanced at me, then at Juliette, then back at me again. "Oh, that's okay," he said. "They're probably riding go-karts or something

I'm not really into. I could hang out with you all for a little while longer."

"Really?" I said. I couldn't believe my luck! "That's great! What should we ride next?"

Kiki pointed to the Ferris wheel. "That one!" she cried.

And from then on, the night just got better! I had a permanent partner for all the rides Kiki was too small to go on and that Juliette wasn't crazy about trying. And Juliette didn't have to sit by herself on the less crazy rides, when Kiki insisted on sitting with me.

Plus, Nick — thanks to all his baseball playing — was an excellent milk-bottle toppler. He won not one, not two, but three giant, stuffed "matching friendship snakes," as Kiki called them — plus a floppy-eared hound dog we all knew Emery would love.

"Isn't Nick nice?" I asked Juliette as we headed home in the car at the end of the night. There weren't many guys, after all, who would have hung out with three girls like us for so long. Unless . . . they liked us! Did he? Could he? I wished I knew enough about boys to tell if Nick liked me. I am not always accurate on that account, as Liza and Mina would attest. But he sure seemed to.

Especially after that night. In fact, I wondered if after the carnival we were even kind of . . . going out? (Probably not, but I'd say, "Definitely, yes!" if Olivia Miner ever asked me.)

It was funny how life had brought us together in so many ways — on the pier, on our beach, at the carnival. Didn't that mean something? Wasn't that fate?

Plus, we had so much in common. I'd already started a list in my head:

- Loves the beach.
- Loves to surf.
- Loves music.
- Not bad at cloud-spotting.
- Loves cotton candy.
- Hates go-karts!

I thought about maybe asking Juliette what she thought, sometime when Kiki wasn't around and my mom and dad weren't totally *eavesdropping* from the front seat of the car.

"Don't you think he's nice?" I asked again.

"Yeah . . . he is," Juliette said softly.

"He should wear clothes all the time!" Kiki chimed in.

Chapter Eleven

A taxi came the next day to take my dad to the airport.

"Now, don't forget," he told me, tossing his bag into the backseat, "starting tomorrow, you can watch me online."

I shook my head. "Dad, we don't have Internet. Remember?"

"Oh, that's right. Too bad for you." He grinned. "Well, sunshine, enjoy all this sunshine while you have it. If this hurricane maintains its trajectory, you're going to be looking at substantial precipitation and gusts of up to thirty knots in, oh, about seventy-two hours."

"Dad, can you not talk like a weatherman for *once*?" I groaned.

He laughed. "Okay. There's a lot of wind and rain coming your way."

"Thank you." I looked up at the sky, which was as clear and blue as ever. There wasn't even a cobweb of a cloud. "I'll believe it when I see it," I said, mostly because I knew that would drive my dad bonkers.

"Hey!" He held his hands out to the side. "Who's the most trusted name in weather?"

I rolled my eyes. "Mack Macintosh."

"You bet your weather vane," he said.

"But we're not going to get a real hurricane up here, are we?" I asked him.

"No, no, no," he said. "It'll just be a storm by the time it gets up here. If it was a real hurricane, they'd make you evacuate." He looked at the old house behind us. "They might make you evacuate, anyway," he joked.

"Not funny, Dad," I said.

"Sorry." He wrapped me up in a big hug. I thought of Juliette's dad, and was so glad to have my own dad right there that I hugged him back even harder.

"I love you, Dad," I said. "I'm really going to miss you."

*   *   *

131

Mack Macintosh is not the most trusted name in weather for nothing. Did it rain, oh, about seventy-two hours after he left? Did it ever! Buckets. And barrels. Herds of cats and packs of dogs. And was it loud! Imagine the sound of marbles beating on the roof, and multiply that by two whole days! Then there was the wind, roaring like a train, spraying sand and water through every crack in the old house. I'd never been in a hurricane, and after a storm like that one, I never wanted to!

How could my dad go chasing them? I was pretty sure he was certifiably insane.

Thank goodness I suggested we get more flashlights and candles before it started raining, because it didn't take long at all for the power to go out. With all the shutters battened down, the house was like a giant tomb: stuffy and stinky and as dark as dirt.

And where was Josh, the Boy Scout, while I was preparing us for the worst? Tying a key to our kite and running out to play Ben Franklin, of course. (Don't worry. There wasn't any lightning or thunder — yet. And my mom threatened to drive him straight to Grandma Macintosh's if he didn't come back inside right away.)

We spent a lot of our time running around with pails and buckets, pots and pans, and whatever else we could find, trying to catch all the leaks in the house's lame excuse for a roof. The rest of the time we spent running around again, emptying them out.

"Too bad we didn't get around to fixin' the roof yet," said Karen. Her tone was more nervous than I, personally, would have liked to hear. "Do you think it's gonna hold?"

Jay wrapped her in his arms. "It'll be fine," he assured her. "*Hakuna matata*. Right, kids?"

"Er . . . right. If you say so," I muttered.

But then came day two.

Then it wasn't the roof that collapsed; it was us. You'd think that in a big, giant house, there'd be enough room for ten people. And maybe if two of them weren't Josh and Brian, there would be. But we were not so lucky. After one day trapped in the house, Josh and Brian began to get bored. And when Josh and Brian got bored, it wasn't pretty.

You couldn't think about doing a puzzle, because they would "accidentally" knock into the table, messing up what you had done and losing half of the loose pieces.

You couldn't think about playing a board game, because they would "accidentally" shoot Nerf rockets into your board, losing your place and ruining the whole thing.

You couldn't think about playing Polly Pockets with Kiki, because they would "accidentally" run up and ask which one was you and which was Jeremy Ryan and where you were going on your "hot date" (when, in fact, it was Nick, and we were going to a movie, thank you very much).

You couldn't think about playing hide-and-seek in what was very probably the best hide-and-seek house in the whole world, because Josh and Brian would grab your ankles when you ran by and drag you under the bed.

You couldn't even think about trying to master "Under the Boardwalk" on the guitar with Jay, because Josh and Brian would walk by with their hands over their ears, wailing and moaning and pretending to be tortured. (If only I could have tortured them!)

And you couldn't even go to your mom and say, "Mom! You have to do something about Josh. He's driving me insane!" because your mom would say, "I'm sorry, Sam, but I think you kids are big enough to work this out yourselves. Can't you see Jay and Karen and Jackie and I are in the middle of a game of hearts? Oh, and will you please empty that bucket?" And you wouldn't even be able to interject, "My name is *Samantha*!" because you'd be so utterly, totally enraged.

And you couldn't, as a last resort, go and sic Emery on them, because as soon as she got "Ruff-Ruff," the stuffed carnival dog, she lost all desire to be a dog herself. Instead, she tied a jump rope around his neck like a leash and dragged him around like she was his master. Unleashing a stuffed dog on two boys had a limited effect.

You couldn't even give up and just go to sleep, even though it was pitch-black all day long, because it was louder than a heavy-metal concert up there in the bedrooms, near the roof. (Rock on, Mother Nature!) Plus, if you closed your eyes, you'd keep wondering if the storm would whip through and blow you out to sea by the time you opened them again.

It seemed like day three would *never* come.

But it finally did.

The rain didn't stop then, but it did fall much more gently, and the wind died down to a soft, steady *whish*. To everyone's relief, we could open the shutters again. Who cared if the light that came in was gray and gloomy? It was fresh and cool, and felt almost like air-conditioning!

I was dying to go outside, but my mom said that if I went out for a walk, I had to take Josh and Brian with me.

"I'll stay in," I quickly said.

I figured I should wait for Juliette to get up, anyway, but by the time she woke up, it had started raining again — hard. It looked like another day of hiding Josh's and Brian's Nerf guns and playing Kiki's Pretty Pretty Princess game.

"Okay, here's the thing," I patiently tried to explain to Emery when we sat down to play. "Only four people can play this game. And if Ruff-Ruff plays, then one of us" — I pointed to her, Kiki, Juliette, and me — "has to sit out."

"I'll sit out," said Juliette.

I crossed my arms and flashed an oh-no-you-don't look at her.

She smiled. "Don't worry. I'll come back," she said. "But I want to go call my dad."

Why hadn't I thought of that?

"Okay," I said, "but hurry. I have to call my dad, too."

She waved and skipped out of the Buoy Room.

"Well, what are we waiting for?" I said as soon as she was out of sight. "Let's spin to see who goes first."

The point of the game was to decorate yourself with matching plastic jewelry. There was a ring, earrings, a bracelet, a necklace, plus a tiara to top it all off. The only thing you didn't want to get was the dreaded Black Ring — then you couldn't win, according to the rules. (If you asked me, though, the Black Ring was the best part. I'd give anything for one of my own!)

Ruff-Ruff got off to a strong start, and soon he was one ring away from a win. Then I swooped in, like the princess that I am, and stole the crown from him.

"One more earring and I win!" I said.

Just as Kiki spun a four and started moving toward a bracelet, there was a sound.

Knock-knock-knock.

Someone was at the door.

Who could be out in this weather? I wondered. Had some beach patrolman driven by the house and decided it should be condemned? Or was it my dad surprising us by coming back earlier than he'd planned? Or was it Juliette's dad, Dave? Had he changed his mind and come down to try to work things out with Jackie?

I jumped up. "I'll be right back," I told Emery and Kiki. "Go ahead and spin for me. I've got to see who's knocking!"

I was practically holding my breath as I ran from the Buoy Room to the front hall and swung the front door open.

"Nick?" I gasped. To say I was surprised is putting it mildly.

He was wearing a bright orange lifeguard rain-coat with the hood over his head, but his smile was as bright and white as ever. "Hi, yourself," he said. His eyes drifted to the top of my head. "You look . . . very fancy. I feel a little underdressed."

Huh? I thought. I looked down at the rumpled pajamas I'd been wearing for three days straight. I knew I hadn't brushed my hair yet that day — or my teeth either. But then I spotted the pink plastic ring on my little finger. *Oh no!* My wrist. My neck. My ear. I still had all my princess jewelry on.

"Oh! These!" I said, reaching up and yanking off my one earring and the crown. "Ha. No! We were just playing this silly princess game, that's all. You know how it is with *kids* around. Anyway, shouldn't you be on the beach right now?"

He looked over his shoulder at the steady rain. "Not much of a beach day," he said.

"Oh, right!" I winced. Embarrassing! "Of course the beach is closed! Who would be out on a day like this, right? Not me. Obviously. Because I'm here. Only I guess you *are* out. . . ."

Meanwhile, inside I was thinking, *Relax! Stop acting like such a dork! It's just Nick. And he's just at your house. That's what friends do. It doesn't mean that he likes you any more than that . . . necessarily. Or does it?!*

"Uh, speaking of being out in the rain," Nick interrupted my thoughts (thank goodness!). "Do you think I could come in?"

"Oh yeah! Of course." It finally registered in my brain that even though he was on the porch, the rain was still blowing all over him . . . and me . . . and the whole hall. I jumped back and held the door open. "Come in," I said.

I grabbed my Hershey Bar towel off the banister. "Here, stand on this," I told him.

Then I tried — really hard — to pull myself together. I had to stop acting like I'd never had a sixteen-year-old lifeguard come to see me at my house before (even though I never had). I had to stop reading more into his visit than a friend dropping in on a friend.

"So," I said finally.

He swept his wet hair back with one hand and smiled. "So," he said.

"Have you been surfing?" I asked. There. That was better! Slowly but surely, my cool was returning. "How are the waves? Are you going out now? I was going to walk down if the rain let up later. But let me just run and change — and check with my

mom — and I can go with you! Oh, and if you don't
mind, I'll see if Juliette wants to go, too."

I spun around quickly to run upstairs — but
his "Uh, actually . . ." called me back.

"What?" I said.

"The wind's pretty strong onshore," Nick said.
"I think the waves are too rough for surfing."

"Aw . . . too bad," I said. "Oh, well. So then what
do you think we should do?"

"Well," he said as his face got this new grin
that I hadn't seen before. It was a little more shy
and sideways, and a little cuter, too. It washed
over me like a wave. But then, as waves often do,
it flipped me over and left me sputtering. Because
what Nick went on to say was, "Actually,
Samantha . . . I came to see Juliette."

Excuse me?

"Is she here?" he said.

"Uh, I don't know . . ." I stammered. *Hang on*.
My brain whirred. *Does this mean Nick isn't here to
see* me?

Nick looked kind of puzzled, even a little sad.
"You don't know?" he asked. "Oh. I wondered if
she wanted to, um, go to a movie. Could you
check, do you think?"

Did I think? What I thought was that I suddenly
felt awful. The whole Nick, Samantha, Juliette

equation had just changed — and I had somehow been subtracted.

Okay, it was fine if he didn't *like* like me. I could deal with that (and had before). But I wasn't so sure I could deal with him liking Juliette. She was *my* friend — finally — on this vacation. And we had less than two weeks left!

Besides, Juliette needed a boyfriend like she needed a hole in the head. What she needed was a good friend like me to talk to, to help take her mind off her troubles. Boys only meant more trouble. Plus, she didn't even like Nick — at least, she'd never said so to me. In fact, she'd told me several times how overrated boyfriends could be. *Sending Nick away would be doing her a favor,* I thought.

"I think . . . she's out," I told Nick finally. Then I looked at the floor. I didn't trust myself to look at him.

"Oh, that's too bad." Nick sighed. "Well, will you tell her I stopped by? Here, I'll give you my number. She can call me later, if she likes." He took a pen out of his pocket. "Give me your hand."

I kept my eyes down as he wrote his number on my palm. (Just the idea of it would have made me melt a few minutes earlier!) I looked at it glumly.

"Okay, well, I'll see you later," he said. "Hopefully, the sun'll be out tomorrow."

A dark cloud, meanwhile, enveloped me. Oh, what was I thinking?

I had to admit, I wasn't doing anyone — but me — a favor by sending Nick away. I could only imagine what Liza and Mina would say if I told them about this. I could just hear Liza: "You sneaky devil!" "You'd better not ever do that to me!" Mina would add.

I couldn't *not* run and find Juliette and tell her that Nick wanted to take her to a movie, I realized. Besides, even if I did, that didn't necessarily mean she would say yes. . . .

I took a step forward. "No, wait," I said. Nick's eyes seemed more gray in the dim light of the stormy afternoon. "Maybe she is here," I said. "I mean, this house is so big and all. Sometimes people come and go, and you never know. For all I know, she could be up in her room on the phone with her dad. So I should probably run and check."

"Uh, okay." He shrugged. "Thanks a lot, Samantha."

I climbed the stairs and headed down the hall to Juliette's room. Her door was closed, but I didn't hear talking, so I knocked.

"Hey." She opened the door. I was glad to see that she looked happy. Lately, she seemed to be having good conversations with her dad. "What's up? I was just coming down."

"Uh, good," I said slowly, "because there's . . . um . . . there's someone here to see you."

Her eyebrows went up. "Who?" she asked.

"Nick." I tried to sound casual. "He said something about a movie. . . ." I could see Juliette's face get all pale and kind of nervous looking. "Oh, but don't worry," I assured her. "I told him I wasn't even sure you were here."

"You did?" she asked quietly.

"Uh-huh," I said. "So if you want, I'll just go back and tell him that you aren't. I really don't mind at all." I turned to go.

"No!" cried Juliette.

I stopped.

"Don't tell him I'm not here," she said, quickly shaking her head. "Just tell him, um, that I'm in the middle of something." She ran her fingers through her hair and looked down at her T-shirt and boxer-shorts pajamas. "I have to take a shower — I haven't even brushed my teeth! Ask him if he can wait fifteen minutes. No, make that twenty. Wow, this is so weird!" She smiled and bit her lip.

"Yeah," I sighed. "It is."

By the time I got back to front door, Nick was no longer there. His coat was hanging on the door-knob, and I could hear his voice down the hall. "Yes, ma'am. I'd love some iced tea. Thank you." I walked toward the kitchen, following the sound.

"Hey, Samantha, sugar," said Karen. "I hope you found Juliette. Don't tell me she went out in this weather."

"Especially without telling me," said Jackie, who sat between Jay and my mother. "That's all I need."

"No, she's here," I said. "She'll be down in about twenty minutes."

Then Nick gave me a smile so big, it was like the sun had come out again.

"Twenty minutes," said Karen. "Well, I believe that's just enough time for us to learn a little more about you, Nick."

"Pull up a seat, my good man," said Jay.

After dealing with those crazies for a while, I knew Nick was glad when Juliette finally appeared from upstairs. We all turned to see her walk in, looking basically amazing.

Nick stood up and knocked his chair over. "Oops . . . hi!" he said.

I shook my head.

"Nick here was just telling us the most wonderful things about himself," said Karen.

"Seems like he had the idea to take you to a movie," Jackie added.

Nick blushed and nodded.

And then Juliette said the last thing I expected to hear.

"Can Samantha come, too?" she asked.

Chapter Twelve

As it turns out, I did *not* go to the movies with Juliette and Nick.

Why not? For one thing, I still had a Pretty Pretty Princess game to win. And me, be a third wheel on a date? I didn't think so. But I wasn't pouting. I swear. They were going to some sci-fi movie, and I am *so* not into them. And when Josh and Brian heard that Juliette and Nick were going, they totally hitched a ride and went to the movies, too! I could tell Nick was a little annoyed. And Juliette, too. But what can you do?

I actually ended up having a pretty pleasant afternoon. I lost the game, in the end, to Princess Ruff-Ruff, but I won a game of hearts with the adults. And I finally got a chance to practice "Under the Boardwalk" with Jay. (And if I do say so myself, it was sounding pretty good!)

Not that it was easy to "lose" both Nick and Juliette. But by the time they got back — and Nick stayed for dinner — I realized that in a way I still had them both. In fact, I now had a *lot* more to talk about with my friend Juliette. Plus, I could see it wouldn't have worked out *romantically* between me and Nick. He loved mushrooms! Blech!

A few days later, my dad arrived — with the sun. Hooray! And before I knew it, we were counting down the days until we went home. Boo-hoo!

Karen and Jay had announced that since the Drift Inn had survived the storm, it was a sign that they should keep the house (ants, mildew, and all) and fix it up. We even started a couple of projects — like washing windows and repainting the DRIFT INN sign — but when I realized they were just making the days go by faster, they started to seem a little less fun.

I honestly couldn't believe that the summer was almost over. By our last week, some of the lifeguards had even left to go back to school. (I was so glad Greenwood Middle School didn't start until September!)

Juliette and I were both glad that Nick didn't have to go early — her for the obvious reason, but me because it meant that he was around and came by one Wednesday night, just as we were finishing off a huge pot of spicy shrimp on the back porch. (Just for the record: I still hated seafood . . . but shrimp were pretty good.)

Naturally, I assumed he was there to get Juliette and take a walk. They were pretty cute when they did that (though I had to admit that I was jealous the first time). But on that Wednesday, it turned out Nick was not there to get Juliette. He was there to get all of us.

"Come on, you all have to see this," he said. "The turtles are hatching down the beach!"

"Turtles?" said my dad.

"No way!" I exclaimed. "Come on, hurry!"

Nick had already told me more about the LOG-GERHEAD TURTLE NESTING AREA sign that I'd seen. It marked a nest full of eggs that a female turtle had laid back in June. There was usually at least one nest found on the beach every year, and the town was careful to protect them since those sea turtles were an endangered species.

We grabbed a few flashlights for when it got dark, plus a few folding chairs for my mom and the "girls" (*old ladies*, if you asked me), and made our way as fast as we could down the beach. A small crowd had already gathered, along two lines of bright orange tape that formed an aisle from the nest to the water. A few people in yellow TURTLE PATROL hats were keeping everyone quiet. As I joined them, I felt a lot like a cheerleader waiting for the football team to run out.

Everyone was good about letting the smallest kids, like Kiki and Emery, sit up near the front. I stood back a little, next to Juliette and Nick. I was relieved to see that we hadn't really missed anything yet. The nest still looked like a rough, shallow sand pit.

But then I looked more closely.

It was moving! In fact, before long it almost looked like boiling quicksand in some movie. Then, after a few more minutes, something small but solid appeared. It was smooth, and dark . . . and had eyes. A tiny turtle head!

And then there was another, and another, and suddenly a bunch — popping up all over the pit like magic!

"Shhh," warned the Turtle Patrol as everyone breathed, "Ooh!" and "Ahh!"

Then the cutest thing happened: The first

turtle's little front flippers came up! They were an inch long, at most, and they waved around, reaching and pulling until the baby turtle was out of the hole. Then it was a free-for-all!

The little sand pit completely gave way and there were suddenly tiny heads and flippers everywhere! They kept flailing and flapping around, climbing up and over one another. If I hadn't known they were turtles, I might have thought they were crazy bugs. And they didn't stop. It was literally a turtle *eruption*. They just kept coming . . . and coming . . . and coming, as if from nowhere. There must have been hundreds! As soon as they were out, they started motoring straight toward the ocean. No looking around, thinking, "Oh! Check out all these people," or "Ahh, smell that salt air." No nothing but "Out of my way! I've got to get to the water now!"

It was weird, though. The turtles were so tiny, and so helpless in so many ways. If a seagull had been around, it would have gobbled them right up. The second a wave reached them, it washed their thumb-size bodies out to sea. But at the same time, they were so sure of themselves, so fearless, and so independent. They *wanted* the wave to take them. And after their awkward shuffle down the beach, I bet being swept away was a relief for them.

I wondered if they were scared at all, but just didn't want to show it — especially with all the people around and a video camera rolling. (I hoped they put it up on YouTube!) I wondered if they'd meet their mother one day, and if they'd know her if they saw her. And I wondered if they'd ever come back to this beach to lay a few hundred eggs of their own. . . .

"Bye-bye, baby turtles," I couldn't help but whisper. "Good luck!"

After that, there was only one good thing about the summer ending: getting Liza's package! It not only included a picture of her dressed as Elvis — hilarious! — but a crazy little cowboy lizard that looked pretty awesome next to the hula-girl lamp in my bedroom. Too bad they had to split up so soon — they made such a cute couple.

Plus, Liza said in her card that she had a *lot* to tell me. She really knew how to torture me. Ugh! But it did give me at least one reason to want to get home.

"So, do you think you'd like to come back next

summer?" my mother asked me as we spent our last afternoon lounging on the sand.

"Yes!" I said at once. "But only if Juliette comes, too," I added. And I was pretty sure she'd want to (especially if Nick was still lifeguarding). Maybe she and Nick would even get *married* one day. The ceremony could be at the Drift Inn. And I could be the maid of honor, since I introduced them!

"Hey," I said to my mom as another idea popped into my head. "What would y'all think if I invited Liza and Mina next year?"

"'Y'all'?" My mom smiled. "You know, you're starting to talk like Karen! But yes, we could ask. That could be fun. There's definitely room."

That night, we had a bonfire on the beach (which honestly worried me with Josh and Brian around, but it turned out okay), and Jay and I played "Under the Boardwalk" for everyone, plus another song that he helped me write. I think it pretty much summed up how I was feeling:

Stay summer, stay, never, never go away.
Summer stay, summer stay, summer stay.
Oh, but I know, I know you gotta go.
I wish it were not so, but I know . . . yeah, I know.
All I can do is write this tune for you.

See you soon, summer. . . .
Summer, see you soon.

Jay was a really good guitar teacher, BTW, though he did tell me that playing the bass was even more fun. Maybe I'll ask for one of those for my birthday *next* year.

And who knows? Maybe next year I'll get a lifeguard boyfriend of my own. . . .

check out the other books in the candy apple summer trilogy!

ENJOY THIS SPECIAL SNEAK PEEK AT

Wish You
Were Here,
Liza

BY ROBIN WASSERMAN

Location: 35,000 feet above Ohio
Population: 347 passengers, 23 flight
attendants, 2 pilots, 1 yapping
Chihuahua in the carrier under
the seat behind me
Miles Driven: 0
Days of Torment: 1

"In the event of an emergency landing, your seat cushion can be used as a flotation device," the flight attendant announced as we took off.

I wanted to raise my hand. *I have an emergency,* I would have said.

I'm on the wrong plane.

On the wrong trip.

In the wrong family.

Stuck in the wrong summer.

Just lend me a parachute, I would have said, *and I'll get out of your way.*

I used to like airplanes. The taking-off part was fun, like a lame amusement park ride. The food was gross, but there was always dessert — cookies or pretzels or candy bars — and, unlike at home, I was allowed to have as much as I wanted. There were people to eavesdrop on, bad movies to watch, and, if I was lucky, a pair of gold wings that I could pin to my backpack. It was pretty much the greatest thing ever.

At least, that's what I thought when I was a kid.

Turns out I was kind of a dumb kid.

Don't get me wrong. The plane wasn't the problem. Not the *whole* problem, at least. Yes, it smelled like BO. Yes, lunch was two pieces of stale bread with watery mustard smushed between them. (There was no way I was going to eat any of the other stuff they gave us.) Yes, the Chihuahua in the carrying case shoved under the seat behind me *Would. Not. Stop. Barking.* But I could have handled all that. *If* we'd been flying somewhere acceptable. Like Hawaii. Or Florida.

Or home.

I closed my eyes, trying to imagine that.

If I were home, I'd be at the local pool, stretching out in the sun, wondering whether Lucas McKidd would notice my new purple bathing suit. Or I'd be figuring out what to wear on the first day of camp. A counselor-in-training had to look the part. I would make my best friends, Sam and Mina, come over and —

That's where the fantasy cut off, like someone unplugged the power cord. Even if I *were* home, Sam and Mina wouldn't be there. Mina was at art camp and Sam was at the beach. They were both away for the whole summer — just like me.

Location: Cheap-O Car Rental, Chicago, IL
Population: 2.8 million
Miles Driven: 0
Days of Torment: 1 (felt like 100)

There were a few small problems with the Great Gold Family Summer Vacation. For one thing, there was nothing great about it. For another, it wasn't technically a Gold family vacation. At least, it wasn't *just* the Gold family.

When I was little, we went on a lot of trips with my parents' friends, the Kaplan-Novaks and the Schwebers. And now that family vacation was back, the Kaplan-Novaks and the Schwebers were back, too. And so were their kids.

We met them at the car rental place by the airport. The office was as old and crumbly as the guy behind the counter. While my parents filled out forms for our rental car, I grabbed a paper cup of lukewarm water and ducked outside. The Kaplan-Novaks were waiting. I hadn't seen them in four years, but they were exactly like I remembered.

"Isn't this awesome?" Dillie said to me right away.

I looked around. There were junky cars, tired tourists, heat waves rising from the black cement — but definitely no awesomeness. "Um, what?"

"This!" Dillie rocked back and forth on the balls of her feet. "I've been so psyched for this trip. I can't believe we get to go away for the *whole* summer. It'll be just like the old days." She tapped her backpack. "I spent the whole flight reading about

Route 66. Like, did you know it crosses eight states and three time zones? And we're going to see them *all*! Awesome, right?"

"Right. Totally." I was starting to get that feeling in my stomach. Like last summer at the amusement park when I'd eaten one too many bags of cotton candy.

"Of course, Roswell — that's Roswell, New Mexico, UFO capital of the world — it's not actually *on* Route 66, but Naomi and Peter — that's my mom and dad; I call them Naomi and Peter, or sometimes Professor Kaplan and Professor Novak, which is kind of a joke, except they don't think it's funny. Anyway, they promised we could take a side trip to Roswell. Won't that be cool?"

You never know, Mina had told me at our "See Ya Soon" party. (Because best friends never say "good-bye.") *Maybe you'll like them.*

Yeah, Sam had added. *You might decide to trade us in for new best friends.*

You've got nothing *to worry about*, I thought, missing them already.

ENJOY THIS SPECIAL SNEAK PEEK AT

by DENENE MILLNER

There were a million people rushing down the street that first morning — so many it made me woozy.

There were moms with their kids, teenagers with their friends, and people with briefcases, some in suits, others dressed in casual summer gear — all of them moving like a wave headed toward the start of their day. I struggled to keep up with Auntie Jill, who was practically leaping down Fulton Street.

"Pick it up, Mina," she said easily while she breezed through the crowd headed toward the subway. I was way behind her, huffing like I was in the middle of a five-mile run. The new art supplies box my mom gave me as a going-away present felt like I was carrying a plump ten-year-old down the street. "If we catch a number four train in the next few minutes, we just might make it to camp early enough for you to see the instructors' artwork in the teachers' gallery."

"Okay," I said simply, because that's about all I could manage as I chased her down the subway stairs and into the cavernous underground station. It was hot down there and it kinda smelled; I was convinced the place was a lab for germ nastiness on the level of the mold experiment we did in science class just before summer break. I made a mental note: *Don't touch anything in the subway.*

Auntie Jill took one look at my face, shook her head, and cracked up. "You'll get used to the subway quicker than you think," she laughed as if she could read my mind. She handed me a small yellow card, then headed for a turnstile leading onto the platform. "Keep your MetroCard in a safe place, okay? You're going to need it to get to all of the different places you and your class will be traveling for your art assignments."

I watched Auntie Jill swipe her card and push through the turnstile, and then I did the same, just as the train rushed into the station. We walked double time to the yellow line, my aunt holding on to my wrist as she squeezed past a couple of people. Standing to my right was a girl about my age, effortlessly hoisting an art supplies box twice the size of mine to look at the oversize hot-pink watch on her left wrist. She caught me staring and smiled. I quickly turned my head toward the opening subway door and moved a little closer to my aunt, who was about to make her move onto the train.

There weren't any seats on the train and because my hands were full with my art supplies and I wasn't used to riding a subway, I forgot to brace myself for takeoff. And what do you know? As soon as the train pulled out of the station, I went flying into the girl with the hot-pink watch.

"Omigod, I'm so sorry," I told the girl, grappling for the silver pole and trying to catch my footing before I fell to the floor. I dropped my MetroCard at the feet of a man with sneakers the size of a small canoe. As I fumbled around on the floor trying to retrieve the card, I could feel practically every eye in the car trained on me. If I had the power to melt into a little puddle and drip out of the cracks of the heavy metal doors, I would have done it, for sure.

"Um, yeah. The poles are a perfect way to keep that from happening again," the girl said as she grabbed my elbow to help me up. She giggled, so I guessed she hadn't meant it to be mean. I cringed. *Nice! As if I'm not already embarrassed enough,* I wanted to say. Instead, I mumbled, "Thanks."

"Here, let me take your art box, honey," Auntie Jill said. "You okay?"

"Uh, yeah, I'm okay," I said, running my fingers over my neon-green miniskirt, swiping at imaginary dirt and trying really hard not to look like a total dork in front of all of New York City.

"Nice art box," the girl said as she moved her hand on the pole to make room for mine. "I saw one just like it at Pearl when my mom took me to buy mine. You an artist?"

I hesitated. I didn't really know what to say back, or even if she expected me to speak to her. And what in the world was "Pearl"? I sure wasn't about to ask her, though, because the girl said it like I was supposed to already know. I settled on a weak "kinda."

"Actually, my niece is quite talented and well on her way to becoming an artist," Auntie Jill chimed in. She clearly couldn't help herself from bragging about me. Embarrassed, I fought back a groan. "I see you have an art box, too — are you an artist?" she asked the girl.

"I want to be." The girl smiled warmly. "I'm actually on my way to the SoHo Children's Art Program. Today's my first day."

"Really? What a coincidence! I'm an instructor there, and my niece Mina is going to be in the camp, too," Auntie Jill said excitedly. "What's your name?"

"Gabriella," she said, rolling the "r" in her name and giving a little wave.

"Well, it's nice to meet you, Gabriella. You look really familiar to me for some reason," Auntie said, tilting her head to the side. I took a closer look at the girl, too; she had an olive complexion and long brown hair pulled into a curly mass at the top of her head.

"Aren't you one of the art teachers at Brooklyn Tech?" Gabriella asked.

"Yes — yes, I am," Auntie Jill said, squinting her eyes as if that was going to help her recognize the girl. "Forgive me, but you don't look old enough for Brooklyn Tech."

"No, no — I don't go to Tech. But my brother does. He's in the science program and takes some of the art classes. I think I've seen you at a few of the art shows there?"

"Oh! Who's your brother?" Auntie Jill asked, the excitement in her voice rising.

"Kent Diaz. He's in the eleventh grade."

"Oh! I know Kent! He wants to be an architect, right?"

"Right," Gabriella said, smiling.

"Well it's nice to meet you!" Auntie Jill said. "See, Mina?" she added, turning toward me. "You're not even at the camp yet and you've made a new friend."

I gripped the pole a little tighter and tossed a halfhearted grin in the girl's direction, then focused my attention on the *Sam* and *Liza* my girls had scribbled on my lucky purple Converses. I'd designed my sneakers on the Converse website all by myself. The funky green stripe up the heel and the starry lavender and neon-pink laces I found at Target made them look super-special. I was wearing them when I got the A on my math final, and when I applied for the summer art camp, which had only fifteen openings, but from what Auntie Jill said, hundreds of applications, so it was safe for me to assume that my sneakers were lucky. Sam and Liza got ahold of them just before we all left for summer vacation and signed their names on the sides with special sparkly white marker, reminding me the entire time they were scribbling not to forget them while I was at my "fancy art camp."

But as for Gabriella? I wasn't sure if she'd be real friend material. Suddenly, I missed Liza and Sam more than ever.